"I am not a dummy!"

Leona shoved Ike and he fell back on the bed. "You are the dummy. Just because your parents are divorced and you have every toy in the universe and you play the cello doesn't mean you can call me dummy."

Leona ran out of the room and down the stairs. She flew past Mrs. Boskowitz and rushed out the door. She didn't close the door behind her, and she didn't care if she never heard David Eisenhower Boskowitz play the cello.

LEONA
······· and ···
ike

by Juanita Havill

illustrated by
Emily Arnold McCully

BULLSEYE BOOKS

ALFRED A. KNOPF • NEW YORK

A BULLSEYE BOOK PUBLISHED BY ALFRED A. KNOPF, INC.

Library of Congress Catalog Card Number: 90-40411
ISBN: 0-679-83278-5
RL: 4.3
First Bullseye Books edition: December 1992

Manufactured in the United States of America
10 9 8 7 6 5 4 3 2 1

Contents

1

What Kind of a Name Is Leona?

"When is Victoria coming back?" Leona climbed up on the kitchen stool, sat down, and planted her elbows on the counter. She watched Mom cut and butter slices of rye bread.

"She just left two days ago," Mom said. "And she'll be gone for three weeks."

"Three weeks! That's too long," Leona moaned. "Why couldn't I go to Aunt Gwendolyn's, too?"

Mom pursed her lips and gave Leona one of her "Now, Leona" looks. "For one thing, Aunt Gwendolyn is not used to having children around. I think she has enough to keep her busy with Victoria. Anyway, I thought you would like being my oldest for a while, Leona."

"I thought so, too," said Leona. She thought she would be glad when Victoria left. She would sleep in the bottom bunk even though Victoria had told her not to. She wouldn't have to listen to Victoria practicing the piano. With Victoria gone, Leona would be the boss over her little brother, Albert.

But for the past two nights, Leona hadn't felt glad. Her bedroom seemed empty, and it was too quiet. She didn't have anyone to whisper to. It was fun to whisper to Victoria. They told jokes and scary stories. Victoria listened to Leona talk about baseball sometimes. Even on nights when Leona didn't feel like talking, she liked to know there was someone else in the room.

As for Albert, he hadn't done what Leona told him—not once. Daddy had to go out of town again. Albert didn't behave at all when Daddy was gone. When Leona told him that she was boss, Albert just said, "No you're not. Mom is."

Leona picked up a bunch of paper clips from a glass bowl on the counter. She hooked them together one at a time in a long chain. "But what am I going to do today?"

"Play with Rita."

Leona shook her head. "Rita says I'm too young." Rita was Victoria's best friend in the neighborhood. Leona played with them sometimes, but only when Rita said so. Without Victoria, Rita wouldn't want to play.

There were other kids in the neighborhood, the Clancy twins and Liza and Aaron, but they were on vacation. Anyway, they weren't best friends with Leona. Leona didn't have a best friend, unless she counted Victoria. Sisters didn't really count as best friends.

Mom arranged the ham sandwiches she had just made in a basket. She added some bars from the cookie jar and a large cluster of red grapes from the fridge.

"I'm going to take this over to the new neighbors," said Mom. "They moved in over the weekend at the duplex two houses down. Want to come?"

Leona wrinkled her nose.

"Or would you rather play with Albert? He's over at the Jacksons' with Ralph," Mom said.

"No way," said Leona. Playing with Albert was like babysitting. "I'll come with you. It won't hurt just to see who the neighbors are."

Mom covered the basket with a tea towel.

Leona stuck the paper clips in her skirt pocket and ran after Mom. When she caught up, she realized she was barefoot. Mom didn't notice.

Mrs. Boskowitz didn't notice that Leona was barefoot either. At least, she didn't say anything when they introduced themselves and she invited them into the living room. Leona was afraid the new neighbor would stare at her feet and say, "I declare, we have a barbarian here," which is what Mrs. Lindahl, the librarian, had said last week when Leona forgot to wear shoes in the library.

Instead, Mrs. Boskowitz seemed to stare at a point on the wall behind them when she wasn't looking at Leona and her mom and smiling. Her smile drooped a little. She had brown hair and blue eyes and lots of freckles over her snub nose. She was pretty, but she looked tired.

"I hope we're not keeping you from your work," Mom said. "Maybe there is something we can help you with, Mrs. Boskowitz."

"Thank you, but the work can wait. I need a break." She smiled and looked at Mom. "Call me Rachel," she said, pouring lemonade into paper cups.

Leona sat with her mom on a small brown sofa. Rachel had unfolded a chair for herself. They set their cups on a card table between them.

Leona looked around the living room. There were boxes everywhere. Yellow boxes, green boxes, boxes with blue lids, and just plain brown cardboard boxes.

"You sure have a lot of stuff," said Leona. She wondered what was in all those boxes. For instance, which ones had toys. Then she saw a huge box with blue letters on the side: WARDROBE. THIS SIDE UP. "What are you going to do with all these boxes after you unpack?"

Rachel looked around the living room and shook her head. "Throw them away. I hope I never see them again."

"Could I have that big one?" Leona pointed to the wardrobe box. "It would make a great playhouse."

"Leona," Mom said, "you should give Mrs. Boskowitz a chance to settle in before you start asking her for things."

"It's all right," Rachel said. "The box is yours, Leona. Maybe you would like to share it with Ike."

"Sure," Leona said, "but who is Ike?"

"I am," a voice said from the stairway behind them.

Leona turned and saw a skinny boy coming down the stairs toward them. He had dark brown hair cut straight above his dark, arched eyebrows. He walked slowly down the stairs like an actor in a play, an actor playing the king. Leona thought he must have been waiting on the stairway and listening to them before he started down.

"My name is David Eisenhower Boskowitz and I am named after a famous president. My friends call me Ike. So does Rachel."

"Oh, you mean your mom." Leona was surprised to hear Ike call his mom by her first name.

Ike looked at her as if she had just told the answer to a riddle before she asked the question. Leona squirmed and wiggled her toes.

Ike stared at her bare feet. He walked slowly over to his mom and said, "I thought you said this neighborhood was civilized, Rachel."

Rachel put her arm around Ike's shoulder and acted as if she hadn't heard him. "Mavis, this is my son, Ike. Ike, Mavis Hanrahan and her daughter Leona."

"Hi, Mavis," Ike said, and shook hands with Mom. Mom smiled and said, "Hi."

Ike turned to Leona, stuck his hands in his pockets, and stared at her. Leona fidgeted. She didn't want to shake hands with him anyway.

"What kind of a name is Leona?" he said.

"It's my name," said Leona. "It used to be my great-great-grandmother's. She came all the way from Ireland in a little boat and Daddy said she used to make the best whiskey in DuPage County."

Mom stood up. "I know you're busy. We ought to go now. If you need any help or information, just call me." Mom wrote her phone number on the back of a coupon she found in her pocket and handed it to Rachel.

"Thanks for stopping by," Rachel said. "And thanks for the lunch basket. I think Ike and I are going to like this neighborhood."

"If you need help unpacking, maybe Leona could come over later," Mom said.

Leona thought Mom was just saying that to be nice, but Ike said suddenly, "How about after lunch? You could eat with us now."

Leona couldn't believe it. This strange, skinny boy who thought she was uncivilized and wouldn't even shake hands with her had just invited her to stay for lunch.

"Thank you, Ike," said Mom. "Don't you think that's a nice idea, Leona?"

Leona could tell Mom wanted her to stay. She tried hard to think of something important she had to do, but she really didn't have anything else to do today. Then she thought of her brother. "Maybe I should go home and have lunch with Albert."

"Albert's having lunch with Ralph," Mom said.

"Then why don't you stay, too, Mavis?" Rachel said. "You've brought so many sandwiches. We can picnic right here in the living room."

Rachel nodded toward the basket. Ike picked it up and offered Mom and Leona sandwiches.

Leona stared at the basket for a minute. Then she chose a bunch of grapes and half a sandwich. If she had known she was going to have to eat one of these sandwiches, she would have told Mom to make peanut butter.

2

David Eisenhower Boskowitz

Leona concentrated on her grapes. She snatched a look at Ike to see what he was doing. He was concentrating on his grapes, too. He dangled the fat red grapes by the stem and plucked them off one at a time.

Leona noticed that Ike had long thin fingers, just like Victoria. She wondered if he played the piano, too. She hadn't seen one here in the living room. Maybe a piano was in one of those giant boxes.

"It's fun to have new neighbors, don't you think, Leona?" Mom said.

Rachel smiled. Ike didn't say anything. Neither did Leona. She was thinking that it depends on who the neighbors are. She was afraid Ike might be like Kevin Stoner. Leona had sat by Kevin Stoner for two whole months in third grade. When they traded papers to mark them, Kevin Stoner put a check on all Leona's mistakes before the teacher gave the answers. Then he drew a sad face on her paper before he handed it back. Leona would like to have a friend in the neighborhood, but someone like Kevin Stoner could never be her friend.

When Mom got up to leave, Leona was still picking the crusts off her sandwich. Rachel walked Mom to the door. Ike finished eating and got up.

"Hurry up," Ike said, running up the stairs.

"But I'm not done yet," Leona said, dropping a handful of bread crusts into the sandwich basket.

"What's keeping you?" Ike whined from upstairs.

"I'm coming," Leona said.

Ike stood by his bedroom door. He turned his palm up and pointed to the room with a sweep of his arm, like a game show host. "This is my room," he said as if nobody else in the world could have a room like it.

Leona could tell that Ike was waiting for her to say something about his room. It made her uncomfortable, as if she were opening a birthday present from someone who couldn't wait to see if she liked it. In that case, she usually didn't.

Ike's room wasn't bad. For one thing, it was big. And he didn't have to share it. The walls were blue and the curtains were darker blue with pictures of constellations on them. Except for some cardboard boxes stacked against one wall, the room was neat.

Too neat, Leona thought. When people move, it's supposed to be messy. The double bed was made. At the foot were plastic baskets filled to the brim. Leona could see a compass and two flashlights on top. There were games: Scrabble, Mousetrap, chess, and Chinese checkers. She wanted to start digging through the baskets to get a better look, but she didn't know where to begin.

"Did you make all those models?" Leona pointed to a shelf of boats and cars and airplanes.

"Of course," Ike said. "With David."

"Is David your best friend?" Leona asked.

"No, dummy. He's my dad."

"You don't have to act so smart," Leona shouted back. "I didn't know." How was she supposed to know that David was Ike's father? She hadn't even known who Ike was until this morning. She had a horrible feeling that Ike was going to be worse than Kevin Stoner.

On the other side of the bed against the wall was a case for a fat guitar and a music stand like the one Mr. Rose, the music teacher, had at school.

"Do you play the guitar?" Leona said.

"That's a cello," Ike said. He didn't actually say "dummy" but Leona heard it in his voice. "I played the cello with the Youth Symphony. I don't know where I'll play now. You probably don't have a Youth Symphony here."

"We don't need one," Leona said. She wasn't sure what a Youth Symphony was, but her town was fine the way it was. "My sister plays the piano," Leona said. "Her name is Victoria and she has lots of talent."

"Hmm," Ike said, unimpressed.

Leona stared again at all the things Ike had in his room. "You must be rich," she said. "That means you're spoiled. My dad always tells us that we wouldn't want to be rich or else we would be spoiled rotten."

"I'm not spoiled," Ike said. "I'm not rich either. David is rich," he added. "Rachel says we can manage without him."

"Without him?" Leona said. "Where did he go? Is he dead?" Even if Ike was spoiled, she would feel sorry for him if his dad was dead.

"No," Ike said, taking a large blue box from a shelf. "He and Rachel are divorced." Ike shoved the box at Leona. "Want to see my coin collection? Here." He took the lid off the box.

There were dark blue books inside. Leona lifted up the top one and opened it. Every thick cardboard page was filled with quarters, real quarters stuck in little pockets in the page.

"You are, too, rich. Look at all these quarters."

"They're not for spending. It's a collection."

"Why do you want to put all these quarters in a book? You could buy something instead. Anyway, they all look the same."

"They aren't the same. Some are from different years. They aren't in the same shape," Ike explained.

"They all look round to me."

"Of course they're round, dummy. 'Shape' means 'condition.' Some are in better condition than others."

Leona gripped the book hard to keep from punching Ike. "I am not a dummy. So quit calling me one."

Ike jerked the book from Leona and plopped it back in the box. "I collect other things, too," he said, but he didn't reach to show Leona. "Stamps and rocks and fossils. What do you collect?"

Leona put her hand in her skirt pocket. She felt the paper clip chain and began to turn it around and around. "I collect glass animals." Leona lied about the collection, which really belonged to Victoria. "I have a very rare glass monkey." She didn't say that it had come from a box of tea bags. "And I collect baseball cards. I have all of the Chicago White Sox."

"Baseball is dumb," Ike said.

Leona was beginning to think that "dumb" was Ike's favorite word. Maybe he was dumb himself. Leona pulled the paper clips from her pocket and dangled them in front of Ike.

"I collect paper clips," she said. "And they are all alike, just like your dumb quarters."

"I collect paper clips, too." Ike reached out and Leona jerked the paper clips back, away from his fingers. "But they're at David's office," Ike said.

Good, Leona thought. Then she wouldn't have to look at them. She had been joking about the paper clips, anyway. Couldn't he tell?

Leona put the paper clips back in her pocket. "Do you want me to help you unpack this bag?" She reached for the metal clasps on a brown suitcase by the closet door and started to open them.

"Don't touch it!" Ike yelled. "That one always stays packed."

"Why?" Leona said. "Are you going to run away?" She used to keep her lavender straw purse packed with things to take when she ran away. Except she had changed her mind and decided to stay with her family after all.

"That's my suitcase for going to David's. I go every other weekend."

"Oh," said Leona. She looked at the suitcase. It was just like the one Daddy had taken on his trip to Minnesota. She missed Daddy. She wished he would come back soon. She wouldn't like Daddy to live someplace else.

"Why did your parents get divorced?" Leona asked.

Ike sat down on his bed. "I don't know." He shook his head and looked at the floor as if maybe he did know but he didn't want to tell. Finally, he said, "They yelled at each other a lot. In fact, they argued all the time."

"That must have been tough," Leona said. "I hate for grown-ups to argue. Once Mom and Daddy had a big argument about washing windows. Daddy said to use wadded-up newspaper to clean the windows, and

Mom said ammonia and vinegar in warm water worked better. I thought the windows looked all right either way."

"Rachel and David didn't wash the windows," Ike said. "That was never a problem. I think that divorce all starts when your dad is gone a lot."

Leona felt uncomfortable talking about dads being gone a lot. She didn't want to hear any more about divorces right now.

"Aren't you going to play your fat guitar?" Leona said.

"My what?" Ike jumped off the bed and looked at Leona as if she had thrown up on his floor. "It isn't a fat guitar, dummy. It's a cello. How could anyone be so stupid?"

Leona jumped up. "I am not a dummy." She shoved Ike and he fell back on the bed. "You are the dummy. Just because your parents are divorced and you have every toy in the universe and you can play the cello doesn't mean you can call me a dummy."

Leona ran out of the room and down the stairs. She flew past Mrs. Boskowitz and rushed out the door. She didn't close the door behind her, and she didn't care if she never heard David Eisenhower Boskowitz play the cello.

3

Ike and His Big Mouth

"I hate Ike." Leona stomped into the kitchen. "David Eisenhower Boskowitz is stupid and dumb. I wish he never moved into our neighborhood."

Leona's mom was standing on the kitchen stool taking spice jars from a shelf and setting them in a cardboard box.

"Leona, you sound very upset," Mom said. Then she lowered the box toward Leona. "Here, help me with this."

Leona grabbed the box and set it on the floor.

"I thought you wanted someone to play with." Mom climbed back down to the floor.

"I do," said Leona. "But not Ike. I'd rather play with Albert than with Ike."

"Maybe you need to give Ike some time. After you get to know him, you might become friends."

"Friends!" Leona said. "With Ike?" Ike is too different from me, she thought. Friends are supposed to like the same things. Leona wasn't very interested in coins and stamps, or even playing the cello. And Ike had said that baseball was dumb. How could Leona be friends with anyone who thought baseball was dumb?

Friends are supposed to be nice to each other, too. Ike hadn't been nice to Leona at all.

"Ike's mean," Leona said.

"Why? What did he do, Leona?"

"He kept calling me 'dummy.' He acted like he's so important and I'm stupid."

"He shouldn't have done that," Mom said. "But maybe he's mixed up by the move. He needs time to get used to everything."

"I don't know," said Leona. "I just wish he hadn't come. Why couldn't a nice nine-year-old girl who likes baseball move there instead?" And, Leona thought, she should like all kinds of animals and not be afraid of climbing trees or going full speed on a bicycle. She would be a best friend. She and Leona would go everywhere together, and when they weren't together, they would talk on the phone, just like Victoria and Rita.

But a nine-year-old girl didn't live in Ike's house. Ike lived in Ike's house. Every time Leona rode her bicycle to the park, she would have to ride past his house. She could even see his backyard from her backyard.

"I wish I never had to see him again."

"Leona," Mom said sharply. She pulled a plastic bucket from under the sink and tossed a fat yellow sponge beside it. "Moving is not easy. You've always lived here, in the same house. You don't know how hard it is for Ike to come to a new neighborhood. You should talk to Daddy about moving. Grandpapa worked for the railroad and Daddy moved seventeen times when he was a boy. Grandmama Hanrahan said he was quite a handful. Every time they moved someplace new, he got into a fight."

"Daddy?" Leona said. Leona couldn't understand why moving could make someone mean. She *had* lived in the same house all her life. She had never even gone to a different school. She always thought it would be fun to move. Moving would be like going on a long vacation with her family, except they wouldn't come back to their old house. Maybe Leona would miss the tree in the backyard and her big closet, but it wouldn't make her mean.

Besides, if Daddy hated moving, why was he going on all of these trips? Leona remembered what Ike had said. If only he hadn't said anything about how divorces get started when dads go on trips.

"Why does Daddy keep leaving us, anyway?"

"He's not leaving us, Leona. He's on a business trip. It's for his work. He has a lot of it at the moment and that's good."

"But aren't you worried, Mom?" Leona said.

"Worried?" Mom poured ammonia into a bucket as she filled it with hot water. White bubbles foamed near the top of the bucket.

Leona blinked her eyes, and Mom sneezed.

"Oh, I always worry a little when he takes the plane," Mom said. "But that's silly. Do you know, it's much safer to fly than to drive on the Kennedy Expressway at rush hour?"

"I didn't mean that kind of worried," Leona said.

Mom frowned at Leona. "What kind of worried did you mean?"

Leona didn't have the words for the kind of worried she meant. Ike probably would. He was the one who told her to watch out when your dad is gone all the time.

"I think I mean the watch-out-something's-going-to-happen kind of worried."

"Hmm. Well, don't let your imagination carry you too far away." Mom plunged the sponge into the bubbly bucket. "Daddy will be home tomorrow. But he might have to make another trip soon."

Another trip, Leona thought. What if it's true? What if Daddy keeps going on trips until he leaves us? Why isn't Mom upset? She should be sad, or at least grumpy. Leona watched Mom squeeze the sponge, mop the shelf, then drop the sponge back into the bucket and then do the whole thing over. She didn't look sad. She looked the same as usual.

"Instead of just standing and staring," Mom said over her shoulder, "maybe you could help, Leona. Take this box of cans for the food shelf donation to the garage."

Leona could see Mom didn't want to talk anymore. Maybe she was trying to get Leona out of the kitchen so she could burst out crying.

Leona carried the box from the kitchen to the step by the garage door. Then she sneaked back inside. She peeked around the cabinet, expecting to find Mom crying into the bucket of sudsy ammonia. But Mom had moved on to another shelf and was humming while she scrubbed.

Suddenly Albert came blasting through the back door. "Look, Leona!" he screamed. "Look what me and Ralph found." He hoisted a piece of rusted metal in front of Leona. "Ralph says it's an antique. It's 'spensive."

"Don't be a dummy, Albert. That's not an antique. That's a piece of junk," Leona said.

"I'm not a dummy," Albert shouted. He let the metal piece drop to the floor and dragged it toward Mom. "Mom, Leona called me a dummy."

"Why, Leona, didn't we just have a talk about how much you dislike having Ike call you names?" Mom said without looking up from her work.

"I'm sorry," Leona mumbled at the kitchen floor. "But Albert called that piece of junk an antique."

"It is an antique. Ralph's mom said I can keep it, too."

Mom looked up. "Oh," she said. "Well, I don't think you should keep it in the kitchen, Albert. Leona, why

don't you take Albert and his piece of . . . antique outside and play for a while."

Leona sat on the bench swing on the front porch.
She told Albert he could sit and swing with her when
he put his junk down. After a while Albert climbed
into the swing. Together they leaned forward and
tilted back. Forward and back, forward and back until
the swing began to move.

"Albert," Leona said. "I think you need to get
ready."

"Ready?" Albert said. He brought his knees up to
his chest and started to stand up.

"Don't, Albert. You're not supposed to stand up,"
Leona scolded. "I was saying that you should get ready
for when Daddy comes home."

"Daddy's bringing me a baseball cap," said Albert.
He crouched on the swing seat, ready to spring up.

"Is that all you think about, Albert?" It was going
to be hard to make Albert think about something besides presents from Daddy. "I'm not talking about
presents. I'm talking about something serious," Leona
said. "Haven't you noticed that Daddy has been gone
a lot lately?"

"Um-hum. He always brings me something." Albert smiled.

"Try to listen, Albert." Leona wished that Victoria
were home. It was hard to be the oldest. It was hard

to figure out what to say. Victoria would know how to tell Albert.

"Albert, do you know what divorce is?"

"Is it on TV? Is it like *Man of Force*?" Albert reached for the swing chains above his shoulder.

"No, it's not on TV. Can you sit down and leave the chains alone? Listen. This is important." Leona waved her hands the way Daddy did when he wanted to make a point. "Divorce is something that can happen to people. It hurts."

"Like an owie?"

"It's not the same as an owie. It makes you sad-hurt."

"Daddy ran over my truck. That made me hurt-sad." Albert stood up.

"Divorce is with people, Albert, not toys. It's when people quit being married. Dads and moms don't live together anymore. It happened to someone who moved into the neighborhood. It could happen to Mom and Daddy."

Albert had grabbed the chains above his head. He looked down at Leona. His big brown eyes looked like the glass eyes of a baby doll. Leona wanted to hug him just then, to hug him and take care of him, no matter what happened.

She reached up to put her arm around him, but Albert climbed up onto the swing back. Just as he did, the swing flipped over. Leona rolled onto the porch, bumped her head, and did a back somersault while Albert landed on his feet with a triumphant smile.

Leona rubbed her shoulder and stood up slowly. "Albert, you're not supposed to stand on the swing or grab the chains."

Before Leona could flip the swing back, Mom was at the doorway. She shouted through the screen, "Can't you play for two minutes without getting into trouble?"

"Leona did it," Albert said.

"I did not." Leona stared hard at Albert. Sometimes if she stared at someone for a long time, she could make them say the truth. But it never worked with Albert. He never budged.

Albert ran to Mom for a hug, but Mom was not in a hugging mood. "Why don't you both cooperate with each other and put the swing back the way it was?" she said and went back to the kitchen.

Leona kept her eyes on Albert while they turned the swing over. "It was not my fault," she snapped at him. Albert had such a hurt look on his face that she added, "Oh, it's not your fault either."

Leona sat back down in the swing. Albert would never understand about divorce. He was too little. Leona wouldn't mention it again. Ike shouldn't have said anything about dads going on trips and getting divorced. He should have kept his mouth shut.

"It's Ike's fault," she said. "Ike and his big mouth."

4

A Box
for Leona

Leona felt grumpy when she opened her eyes in the morning. She couldn't remember what her nightmare was, but she knew she must have dreamed. She kept waking up. Each time she woke, she thought about Ike and his fat guitar. Then she thought about her parents getting divorced.

How could she keep Daddy at home? How could she make Mom understand about his long trips? She and Albert and Victoria would have to be nicer to Daddy. So would Mom. Mom could make corned beef and cabbage for every dinner, and maybe Leona would even eat some.

It would be terrible if Mom and Daddy divorced. Where would she live? And what about Albert? And Victoria?

Leona didn't want to see Daddy on weekends only. He always had chores to do on Saturday. On Sunday he slept too late to go to church. He was more fun on Thursday nights when they watched TV together and

on Friday afternoons. He usually took Friday afternoon off to go swimming or play baseball in the park.

Leona needed to live with Mom, too, so she would
know when to wash and brush her hair and when to
come in for supper. Besides, no one could make an
owie feel better than Mom.

Rrrring! The telephone scattered her thoughts.
Leona sat up and bumped her head on the slats of the
top bunk.

"Ow!" She had forgotten she was sleeping in Victoria's bed while Victoria was gone.

Her head throbbing, she jumped out of bed and
ran to the phone on Victoria's desk. She picked up the
receiver. Before she could say anything, she heard
someone talking. "Hello. This is Ike." She hung up.
Rubbing her head and wondering what Ike was up to,
she crawled back into bed.

Then she heard the creak of stairs and footsteps
coming down the hall.

"Good morning." Mom set a stack of laundered
clothes on the chair by the door. "It's time to rise and
shine."

"I bumped my head. Look how big my lump is."

Clicking her tongue softly, Mom walked over to the
bed. She sat down on the edge and bent over Leona.
"Oh, I bet that hurts." She brushed Leona's hair away
from her forehead and blew on the lump. "Did you
fall out of bed?"

"No." Leona pointed to the slats of the bed above her.

"Maybe you're better off on top. That was Ike on the phone."

"Ike?" Leona said, trying to act surprised.

"He's found another box and would like you to go over to choose which one you want. I told him you could go after breakfast."

"Aw, Mom." Leona didn't think she wanted to see Ike after breakfast. "But I have chores to do."

"You can do your chores later," Mom said.

Leona shook her head. Didn't it occur to Mom that maybe she wanted to do all her chores right after breakfast, except for maybe cleaning the bathroom?

"Remember what I said about Ike. If you're nice to Ike, I think he'll be nice to you."

"He wasn't nice yesterday."

"He might feel sorry about that, and this is his way to make up for it," Mom said.

"I don't know," Leona said. He would probably call her "dummy" again and start talking about divorce, which was the last thing Leona wanted to talk about. But what if Ike brought the box over? What if he talked to Mom about divorce? Then she might start getting ideas, if she didn't already have some. Leona decided it would be better if no one talked about divorce at all. She would have to go get the box to keep Ike from coming over.

"All right. I'll go," Leona said. "But I won't stay and play. I have too many chores to do."

Mom smiled as she stood up. "You're a good sport, Leona."

Leona headed over to Ike's after breakfast. She felt uneasy on the doorstep. The door opened before she rang the doorbell.

"I've been up for hours." Ike waved her into the house. "I called you this morning, and your mother said you were still in bed."

"So what?" Leona stepped inside and looked around for the big box in the living room. It wasn't there. "It's summer. Don't you sleep late in summer?"

"Rachel says I have to get up early. I have stamina in the morning."

Leona wasn't sure what stamina was, but she wasn't going to ask Ike. She thought it might be something to eat. "I have Wrinkle Flakes every morning," she said. "As many as I want."

"Wrinkle Flakes?" Ike seemed interested for an instant. Then he turned and headed for the stairs. "Cereal in boxes isn't good for you."

Here we go again, Leona thought. But she followed Ike up the stairs. At the end of the hall, past Ike's room and his mother's room, were two large cardboard boxes. The bigger one must have been the one Ike called about. It was taller than Leona and wide enough for four kids to stand in.

"Wow! What came in this box? A refrigerator?"

"It's a wardrobe box." Ike tapped it. "For clothes."

"I like it," Leona said. Even if it was Ike's box, it was super. It was so big you could almost live in it. "Are you sure you don't want it?"

"Rachel says all the boxes have to go."

Leona ran her hand down the side of the box. She bent to lift the corners. "It's pretty heavy."

"I'll help you carry it downstairs," Ike said.

"Oh, I don't need help to get it downstairs." Leona tipped the box on its side and began sliding it to the stairs. "I have a quick way to get it down. Albert and I do this with the laundry basket sometimes.

"Is anybody there?" Leona called out. No one answered, so she tilted the box over the top stair and let it slide downward. It whooshed down the steps as fast as the roller coaster at Little America. Leona heard Ike say "Gosh" when the box bumped to the bottom with a hollow thud.

"What happened?" Rachel called as she came down the hall from the kitchen.

"Hi, Rachel." Leona jumped down the steps two at a time.

"Oh, Leona. Hello. I didn't realize you had come."

"I was showing Ike how to get a box downstairs in a hurry."

"I see," Rachel said as if she didn't see at all.

Ike walked slowly down the stairs. "I'm going to help Leona carry the box to her house now. I told you she would choose this one."

Leona was going to say that if Ike wanted it for himself, she would understand, but she was really glad to hear Rachel say, "It's yours, Leona. Don't be too long, Ike. I want you to come with me to the gallery."

Rachel held the front door open as Leona and Ike heaved the box out the door and down the steps. Neither one spoke as Leona pulled and Ike pushed the box down the sidewalk. Leona was thinking that the reason she had gone to Ike's was to keep him from coming over, but that's exactly what he was doing now.

"Okay," Leona said when they got to the back porch. "Just leave it here. I'll have to check to see if Albert is here." She knew that if Albert saw the box, he would want to play in it right away. She had other plans for her box.

She went in the back door. Ike stepped in right behind her. Albert had just wandered into the kitchen. He had an orange tractor in one hand. He rubbed his eyes with the other.

"I want Victoria," Albert said.

"Is she the one who plays the piano?" Ike asked.

"She's my big sister," Albert said. "Who are you?"

Before Leona had a chance to introduce him, Ike

said, "I'm David Eisenhower Boskowitz. I'm named after a famous president. What's your name?"

"I'm Albert." Albert beamed. "After Victoria and Leona."

Ike looked surprised. "How can you be named after Victoria and Leona? Your name is Albert."

"Victoria comes first. Then Leona. Then me. Albert comes after."

Leona felt as if she had to explain. "He's only four, you know. Four-year-olds can be kind of dumb."

"Mom," Albert screamed. "Leona called me—"

"Shh, Albert. I didn't say you. I just said four-year-olds."

Albert closed his mouth and frowned. Then he looked at Ike. "Are you Ike? Ike has a big mouth. Leona said so on the swing yesterday."

Ike looked at Leona. His brown eyes narrowed.

Leona could see that Ike's feelings were hurt. She looked down at her toes and wiggled them in her sandals. She hadn't meant to hurt his feelings.

"I don't care if you have a big mouth," Albert said. He grabbed Ike's hand and dragged him toward the playroom. "Want to see my racetrack?"

"Sure," said Ike. "Is it big? Can we play with it?" Ike walked off with Albert as if he had come over to play with Albert in the first place.

For an instant Leona felt left out. She had met Ike first. She and Mom had taken lunch over to Ike and

Rachel yesterday. They had eaten with them, too. Even if she didn't want to be friends with Ike, she was the one who should be showing Ike around. Leona rushed after them.

"You have to eat breakfast first, Albert," Leona said, but Albert didn't pay any attention to her.

He had already pulled out his semitrailer and the minicar loop racetrack. "I have trucks and racecars. Look, you build things with them," he said. He tried to fasten two pieces of plastic track together.

"Impressive," Ike said. He sank down to his knees and put the pieces of track together for Albert.

Leona ran over and whipped two track sections out of the toy box. She snapped the pieces together expertly. Maybe Leona couldn't play the cello, but she could put that racetrack together faster than anyone in her family. It used to belong to her.

"Do you have an electric train?" Ike asked.

Albert shook his head.

"I do," Ike said while he worked. "I have a gigantic electric set. It hasn't been set up yet."

"Can I see it? Can I see your train?" Albert jumped up.

"Albert!" Leona shouted. She was afraid Albert was going to run over to Ike's. Albert shouldn't get to see Ike's train first. Leona should.

The phone rang. Then Mom came into the playroom. "Time for breakfast, Albert. Your mother just phoned, Ike. She said you have to go to the gallery now."

Ike snapped the last piece of track in place. "I don't want to go with her," Ike said in a low voice. He whizzed a car around the loop so fast it fell off. Then he got up and walked slowly toward the kitchen.

"See you, Albert. See you, Leona." Ike tramped to the back door.

"See you," Leona said. She should have been glad that Ike had to leave. She hadn't wanted him to come in the first place. But she wasn't glad. Instead, she felt let down, the way she did when a baseball game got rained out.

5

Why Isn't Daddy Coming?

While Albert ate breakfast, Leona took the box up to her bedroom. It was big and heavy, but she didn't want to ask Albert to help. Ike had given the box to her, not Albert. If Albert played with the box, he would climb on top of it or roll in it and smash it flat.

Leona pushed the box step by step up to the landing. Then she tried dragging it as she scooted up each step. But the box slipped, and she had to start over from the landing. Finally, she reached the top of the stairs and pushed the box to her room.

Leona cleared a space on the floor of the walk-in closet. It was a wide, wonderful closet. The closet was one of the reasons Leona didn't mind sharing the room with Victoria. She shared the closet with Victoria, too, but Victoria said she was much too old to play in a closet with Leona.

Leona shoved the box across the closet floor, scrunching it against some long dresses hanging at the back. She got her lavender purse, a pillow, her skunk

puppet, and her army flashlight, the one that worked
up to 200 feet under water, and crawled into the box.
She pulled the flaps closed and folded the opposite
corners in to keep them shut.

It was quiet. Leona felt cozy and safe. No one could
bother her here. She took her baseball cards out of the
purse and beamed the flashlight on them. She flipped
through the cards.

"Baseball is not dumb," she said. She was thinking
about Ike. She couldn't help it. She didn't understand
Ike. One day he was worse than Kevin Stoner, and the
next day he gave her a box and helped her carry it
home.

"Leona!" Albert called as he came up the stairs.
"Leona." He stomped into her room.

Leona switched off the flashlight. She hoped he
wouldn't come too near the closet. The door was open
and he might notice her box. He must be close. She
could hear him. She held her breath. She heard Albert
rummaging around in her things. He would probably
take her stuffed dolphin, the one with the zip-open
stomach and the baby dolphins inside. He liked that
one best.

Leona let her breath out slowly, pulled back one of
the cardboard flaps, and looked out. Albert walked
back and forth in front of the closet door. He was
holding the dolphin in his hands. He stopped in front
of the closet with his back to Leona. She could hear
him fumbling with the zipper.

Albert's going to wreck it, Leona thought. "Albert, put my dolphin back," she said out loud.

Albert jumped, and clutched the dolphin tighter. He looked around the room, eyes wide and worried.

"Leona," he whispered. "Where are you?" Then louder, "Leona, come out." Finally he shouted, "Leona, Daddy comes home tomorrow."

"Tomorrow!" Leona shouted. "He's supposed to come home today." She crawled swiftly out of the box and shot out of the closet toward Albert.

Albert dropped the dolphin. "Leona, you were in the closet. Why were you in the closet?"

"Because." Leona closed the closet door. "When did Mom tell you about Daddy?"

"Just now."

"I don't get it," Leona said. "Why did Daddy change his plans? Why didn't he come home when he said he would?" Leona was afraid that something was wrong. What if he didn't want to come home? What if Ike was right about the whole thing? What if Daddy came home and then left right away?

"Albert." Leona grabbed Albert's shoulders. "We have to do something."

"Why?"

Leona remembered how hard it had been to talk to Albert about divorce. She wasn't going to try that again.

"We have to be so nice to Daddy that he won't ever leave again."

"Daddy is nice to me. He is going to bring me—"

"No, Albert, you have to be nice to him."

"I am nice."

"I mean super nice. You have to try to do all the things he likes and not do the things he doesn't like. Don't eat with your mouth open. Don't leave your soldiers in his slippers. Things like that."

"Why?" Albert asked again.

"Because," Leona said. "Because I miss Daddy and I need Mom and I want us all to be together."

"I miss Daddy," Albert said as Leona ran out the door to go downstairs.

"Mom, why isn't Daddy coming?"

Mom was in the kitchen writing a grocery list on a junk-mail envelope. "He had just one more meeting, Leona. Since he won't be able to catch his flight in time, he is staying over. Actually, it works out fine for me."

Leona was stunned. What did Mom mean, "It works out fine"? Daddy was coming home a whole day late and Mom says it works out fine. "It doesn't work out fine. I want Daddy to come home today."

"Oh, so do I. But this way I will have time to finish staining the cupboards in the kitchen. Can you help me with the grocery list? What do we need?"

"We need corned beef and cabbage for supper tomorrow."

"But Leona, you never eat corned beef. You hate cabbage."

"It's Daddy's favorite. You have to fix corned beef and cabbage. I'll eat it. I promise."

"That's thoughtful of you, Leona. But it's really more of a winter meal than a summer one."

"Please, Mom."

"Oh, all right. I suppose we could make sandwiches with the leftover corned beef."

"Yippee!" Leona would never have thought she could be happy about having corned beef and cabbage for supper.

Leona watched Mom write "corned beef" in big rounded letters. Under it she wrote "cabbage" and then "pickles."

"Put 'dress' on your list," Leona suggested. "You need a new dress, Mom."

"From the supermarket?"

"No, you have to go to the mall," Leona said.

"Sorry, but I don't have time today."

"But you can't wear that for dinner when Daddy comes." Leona pointed at Mom's baggy jeans and sweatshirt.

Mom stretched her sweatshirt down over her hips. "I will if I'm going to be in the kitchen cooking the dinner."

Why wasn't Mom being more serious? Leona thought it was very important for Mom to wear a fancy dress for dinner. In her mind she could see exactly what kind of dress Mom should wear. She had seen the dress in one of Victoria's magazines. There was a picture of a man and a woman in fancy clothes sitting at a round table with candles on it.

"Want to come?" Mom folded the list and put it in her purse.

"Not to the supermarket. I have to look for something." Leona ran upstairs to see if she could find Victoria's magazine. When Mom came back from the store, Leona would show her the photo of the man and woman sitting at the fancy table. It would be easier to show Mom the photo than to explain why Mom should dress up for dinner.

6

The Love Letter

Leona found the photo in the February issue of *City Chic*. Victoria had hidden the magazine at the bottom of the drawer because Mom didn't like her to read it. Victoria had probably bought it with her own money. Leona realized she couldn't show Mom the magazine or Victoria would be in trouble. But if Leona cut a picture from Victoria's magazine, she would be in big trouble herself, with Victoria.

Leona read the caption under the photo. "He'll never want to say goodbye." Because of the dinner, she suspected, and because of the dress the woman was wearing. Mom didn't have a gold and black dress like that. Leona turned the pages of the magazine and looked at the other dresses. Mom never wore any dresses like those, either.

Leona stopped when she came to an article called "Love Letters: Love That Lasts Forever." Forever meant a long time. That was exactly how long Leona

wanted Mom and Daddy to stay together. Leona read
the love letters. They were written by famous people,
by poets and writers, and one man who became president, but his name wasn't Eisenhower.

Daddy should write love letters to Mom when he
goes on trips, Leona thought. She knew he didn't because she was the one who usually got the mail, and
there were never any love letters to Mom from Daddy.
Maybe if Mom wrote love letters to Daddy, he wouldn't
go on trips in the first place.

Leona thought suddenly of Ike and his parents.
She wondered if his parents had ever written love letters to each other. Probably not, and now it was too
late. She hoped it wasn't too late for Mom and Daddy.

But Leona couldn't just go and tell Mom to write a
love letter. Mom would think that was strange. She
would have to help Mom secretly. Mom always said
that "the best kind deeds are those done in secret."

Leona took writing paper from the telephone desk
in the upstairs hall. She took several pages in case she
made mistakes. On scrap paper she practiced writing
the way Mom wrote. She wrote "corned beef" and
"cabbage" and "pickles" all over the paper. Then she
copied Mom's signature from her birthday card. She
wrote "Love, Mom" about a hundred times.

Finally, Leona took a clean sheet and began to write
in large, rounded letters:

Dear Michael,
                    I am so glad you
are back. I miss you immensely
when you are absent, my love. I
am fearful and fretting and not
quite the same when you are not
here. Never leave again. Do you
feel as I do? Let's hope we will
always feel this way.
                              Love,
                                Mom

P.S. Write back if you feel the same.
But keep this letter secret. Don't ~~even~~
mention it to anyone, not even me.

Leona put the letter in an envelope, addressed it, and put a stamp on it. Then she drew black wavy lines over the stamp to make it look as if it had come through the mail. Leona hid the letter under her pillow just as Albert wandered into her room.

"I want to play with Ike."

"Ike went with his mom today, remember?"

"Will Ike be home tomorrow? Ike's going to show me his train."

"I don't know," Leona said. "But Daddy's coming tomorrow. We have lots to do." Leona wondered why Albert kept talking about Ike. Probably because of the train set.

The next day Albert pestered Leona to call Ike. Albert wouldn't help her clean the house or make a Welcome Home sign or pick up his room until she told him she would call Ike. She was relieved when she phoned Ike and no one answered. She was too busy to play with Ike today, but she didn't want Albert to go over to Ike's and see all his toys and play there all afternoon.

The mail didn't come until late in the afternoon. Leona and Albert were decorating the Welcome Home sign. Leona ran to the porch to grab the mail from the letter carrier. Then she ran upstairs. She heard Mom in the bathroom taking a bath.

Leona went to her room to sort the letters. She put all Daddy's letters in one stack. On top she put the love letter from under her pillow. She took the mail downstairs and put Mom's mail and the junk mail on the kitchen table. She set Daddy's mail on the desk in his office.

Then Leona ran back upstairs to Mom's room. She had an idea, but she would have to work quickly. She found Mom's jeans and sweatshirt on the bed and grabbed them and threw them down the laundry chute in the hall. If Mom didn't see her old clothes, maybe she would wear something nicer. Leona looked through the clothes in Mom's closet. Didn't Mom have any dresses? Leona found only one dress, a long one with a sash. The dress was yellow with little red flowers on it. She had never seen Mom wear it.

The dress was too long to hang on the closet door-knob, so Leona draped it across the bed. She heard the bathroom door click open and scrambled out of the room. She reached the top of the stairs just as Mom came out of the bathroom. Leona jumped down the stairs three at a time and landed with a thud at the bottom. She sat on the floor for a minute, shaking. She wondered if someday Mom and Daddy would be grateful for the things she had done to keep them together.

Leona was taping the Welcome Home sign above the kitchen doorway when she heard a car pull into the front drive. She rushed out to see Daddy slamming the door of a taxi.

She jumped on him and hugged him as soon as he stepped out. "Welcome home, Daddy! We all love you very much. Mom and Victoria and me and Albert."

"Hello to you, too. How's my Leona? Gee, I missed you."

Leona unhugged Daddy and Albert torpedoed into his arms. "Daddy, Daddy. It's me, Albert."

"Wow! You'd think I'd been gone for years," Daddy said, picking Albert up.

Leona tried to pick up Daddy's suitcase, but it weighed a ton. Daddy set Albert down and took his suitcase. "You can carry this." Daddy handed Leona a shopping bag, and they went inside.

Daddy settled down on the sofa. "Where's Mom?"

"She's taking a bath. And then she's planning a big surprise. We all are."

"I have surprises for you, too." Daddy reached in his sack and pulled out a small wooden airplane and a navy blue T-shirt.

Albert grabbed the airplane and ran in circles around the coffee table. *"Rrrm, rrrm, rrrm,"* he said.

Daddy helped Leona slip the T-shirt over her pink blouse. She tugged it to see the letters. "Minnesota Twins," it said. "Thanks, Daddy," she said. "I have something for you, too." Leona ran to get the letters in Daddy's office. She plopped today's mail on Daddy's lap with the love letter on top.

"Thanks, Leona, but it's probably bills. I'll take care of it later."

"This one looks important." Leona held the love letter in front of Daddy's eyes.

"Hm. So it does." Daddy took the letter. He ran his thumb under the envelope flap, slipped the letter out, and read it.

"Hi, Michael. How was the flight?" Mom came into the living room.

"Oh, no," Leona said out loud, then clapped her hand over her mouth. Mom was not wearing a long yellow dress with red flowers on it. Mom was wearing her green garden pants and a blue shirt with a hippopotamus on the pocket.

"What's wrong, Leona?" Mom said.

Leona shook her head and squeezed her lips together tightly. She couldn't tell Mom that she was supposed to be wearing a dress. Not now. Not in front of Daddy.

"The flight was fine." Daddy stood up and hugged Mom. "But it looks like I'll have to go back soon."

"Oh, no," Leona said again. Hadn't Daddy just read the love letter? What was wrong?

"I won't be gone long," Daddy said to Leona.

Leona felt her eyes wet and runny with tears. She blinked and saw that Daddy's blurry face looked puzzled. Then he smiled.

"Leona, have you been fearful and fretting about something?" He pronounced "fearful and fretting" loudly and slowly, as he looked down at the letter.

What if Daddy read the letter again, out loud, in front of Mom? "Daddy!" Leona shouted. She ran to his side and whispered in his ear, "It's a secret. Don't tell anyone about the letter."

"What letter?" Daddy joked. He folded the letter and put it in his jacket pocket. He patted his pocket and smiled at Leona. Immediately Leona realized that Daddy knew that she knew what was in the letter. She wasn't supposed to, of course, since the letter was from Mom.

Leona knew exactly what Daddy would say next.

"But Leona, how did you know it's a secret?" he said.

"Because." She hesitated. "Because . . . because." Leona couldn't think of a good reason. She couldn't think of any reason at all. She felt trapped. "Oh, no," she said once more.

Daddy reached out to her. Then he sat her down beside him on the sofa.

"What is this all about?" Mom said.

"Everything's wrong," Leona murmured. "Everything's going wrong. Mom isn't dressed up for dinner—"

"Ah," Mom interrupted. "So that's why my old prom dress was on my bed."

"And Daddy is going to leave again. The love letter didn't even work. It's supposed to keep him here forever."

"Love letter?" Mom said.

"I do have to travel again, Leona," Daddy said, "but I'll be back."

"But what if you don't come back?" Leona said. "That's how it happens."

"How what happens?" Mom said.

Leona whispered, "Divorce," as if it were a bad word.

"Leona, where did you get such a wild idea?"

It hadn't seemed like such a wild idea at all. It had

happened to Ike's parents. Divorce was real. "From Ike," Leona said.

"Ike?" Mom said.

"Who's Ike?" Daddy asked.

Albert stopped whirling his airplane around the room. "I like Ike," he said.

"Ike just moved into the neighborhood," Leona said. "His parents are divorced. He told me that when dads go on business trips, that's how divorce starts."

"Oh?" said Daddy. "Well, not with this dad. You don't have to worry, Leona. Maybe Ike was talking about his own dad."

Daddy sounded serious and sure. He squeezed Leona and kissed her on top of the head. She felt warm inside with relief.

Mom hugged Leona, too. "Now I hope you feel better," she said. "Maybe you could tell me where my jeans and sweatshirt are."

"In the laundry," Leona said.

"A good place for them." Mom laughed. "Now, everyone, it's time for a very special dinner. It's your favorite, Michael."

Leona didn't complain, but she was disappointed she would have to eat corned beef and cabbage for no reason at all. Since Daddy was not ever going to leave them, they could be eating tacos.

7

Last One There Is a Rotten Cucumber!

Leona hadn't seen Ike at all over the weekend. He had gone someplace with his father. Now that it was Monday, he was probably back. Leona had been wanting to tell him that her parents weren't getting divorced. Ike had been wrong about the business trips.

In the middle of the morning she went to Ike's house. When Ike opened the door, Leona said, "You are wrong, Ike. My parents aren't getting divorced. You don't know everything."

A hurt look flickered in Ike's eyes and Leona wished she hadn't said anything.

Ike shrugged his shoulders. "I didn't say that your parents were getting divorced."

Leona didn't feel like arguing with Ike, especially since she had hurt his feelings. "Can you come over and play?" she said, to make him feel better. "You can meet Daddy. He's home."

"I'll go ask." Ike left the door open and Leona standing on the front steps.

He came running back. "Let's go," he said.

On the way Leona asked, "Did your dad bring your train set?"

"No. Not yet."

"Is he going to bring it next time?"

Ike wasn't interested in talking about his train.

When they got to Leona's, they went first to Daddy's office.

"I'm David Eisenhower Boskowitz," Ike said to Daddy. "I'm named after a famous president."

"Would that be Dwight Eisenhower?" Daddy shook hands with Ike. "I hear that you have a fantastic train set."

"Oh. Yes, but it's at David's now."

"Ike calls his dad David, instead of Daddy," Leona explained.

"Well, if David ever brings your train to your house, I'd like to see it. So, Leona, are you going to show Ike the rest of the house?"

"Yes. Want to see where I put the box, Ike?" Leona ran up the stairs, and Ike followed.

"This is the best closet in the house," Leona said. "Did you ever see a closet this big?"

Ike stepped into the closet and walked up to the box. "I wish I had a big closet."

Leona was pleased that Ike admitted he liked something of hers.

Leona plunged into the box and turned the weak flashlight beam on Ike as he crawled in.

"I think I might put a window in this box. Right there." Leona beamed the light above Ike's shoulder.

"I can help you," Ike said.

Leona scrambled from the box to get scissors from the shoebox under her dresser, where she kept art supplies.

It took a long time to make the window. "This would be easier if you used an X-acto knife," Ike said in a grown-up way that made Leona feel uncomfortable.

"I have to use these scissors," Leona snapped back, which was true. After she cut a slit in her bedspread by accident, Mom would only let her use sharp scissors on the kitchen table.

"That's kind of dumb, if you ask me," Ike said.

Leona slammed the scissors down. She hadn't liked it when Ike called her names at his house. She didn't like it now. "I made up my mind," she said. "I won't be friends with you if you call me names."

Ike looked surprised. "I didn't call you a name."

"You said I was doing something dumb."

"I didn't say you were dumb."

"Well, you did on Wednesday. Besides, it's the same thing." But Leona didn't feel the way she had felt on Wednesday. She wanted to cut a window in the box and so did Ike. Ike was probably right, too. It was very hard to cut a window with scissors. "Do you want to be friends?" she asked.

Ike picked up the scissors and slowly sawed the cardboard. Leona thought maybe he hadn't heard her. Finally, he said, "Sure."

Leona was glad Ike said that. It made her feel like talking to him about friends.

"Do you have a best friend?" Leona asked. "Where you used to live?"

"Mr. Norton was my best friend. I played chess with him at the library."

"I mean, a best friend you play with all the time, who likes the same things you like."

"Mr. Norton and I both like chess," Ike said. "We played a lot."

Leona supposed that you could be best friends with a grown-up, if you liked the same things. She had never thought about that before. "What about friends your own age?" she said.

"I have friends from music camp. But I only see them in the summer."

"It would be hard to be best friends with someone you don't see all the time," Leona said.

"This year I didn't even see the kids at music camp. I didn't go because we moved." Ike poked at the cardboard. "I didn't want to move, anyway. Nobody asked me if I wanted to move. Rachel and David should have asked me."

Leona agreed. "They should have asked you." Mom and Daddy asked her sometimes about what she wanted: what flavor of ice cream to buy at the supermarket or if she wanted to go to a fancy or a fast-food restaurant. But her parents didn't ask her if she wanted to go to school every day. Some days she didn't really want to. They never asked her if she wanted to go to camp in the summer either. Leona would have liked to go to camp.

"Did you sleep in a tent at camp?" Leona said. "I never went to camp, but we have an army tent. Daddy puts it up in the backyard and we sleep out all night in it."

Ike shook his head. He rolled his eyes upward the way Mr. Rose, the music teacher at school, did when Leona squeaked her recorder. "Music camp isn't in a tent," he said. But he didn't say "dummy." "We have classes in buildings and we sleep in a dormitory. A dormitory is a building, too, with a big room full of beds."

"Leona," Mom shouted up the stairs.

Leona crawled from the box and stood in her doorway to listen to Mom.

"I'm taking Albert with me to the store. Do you think Ike would like to have lunch with us?"

"Yes," said Leona. She forgot to ask Ike.

"Why don't you ask Ike's mom? We'll have lunch when I come back."

"Okay," said Leona. She grinned at Ike. "Now I can show you the backyard. Albert won't be there to bother us."

"I like Albert," Ike said.

Shaking her head in disbelief, Leona led Ike downstairs and out the back door. She showed Ike the junglegym first. She climbed up to the top and hung by her knees.

Ike slowly made his way up the side and sat on the bar below Leona.

Leona skinned the cat and jumped down to run to the maple tree. She grabbed the tire swing with both hands and pulled herself up to the branch on the rope. "This is one of my favorite places," she said. "Come on up."

Ike got as far as the tire swing and stopped. "I like it here," he said.

"Did you ever play skydiver?" Leona yelled. She dangled her legs from the branch before pushing off and dropping to the ground.

"Skydiver? No," said Ike.

"Come on. You can do it from the swings, too." Leona coaxed Ike into a swing and gave him a duck-under push. Then she sat down in the next swing and caught up with Ike in four strong pumps.

"You go as high as you can, and then you jump off," Leona said. "Right at the top." Leona slipped off and shouted, "It's like flying." She slid in the grass when she landed and rolled over and over. "Wow. That must be a record."

Ike's swing started downward. He let go and flew for an instant before landing on his back in the dust.

"Ouf," he said and sat up slowly. He had tears in his eyes.

"That was a good jump," Leona shouted, running to Ike. She pulled him to his feet. "You just got the wind knocked out. It will come back."

Ike brushed dirt off the heel of his hand. "Oh, no. I hurt my hand," he said. "Rachel is not going to like that."

Stripes of blood showed through the dirt on his hand.

"It's just scraped. Come on. I can fix it. I know all about scrapes and cuts." Leona took Ike to the bathroom. She made him hold his hand under the faucet while she ran cold water. "I've had millions of these," she said.

Leona poured liquid from a green bottle onto a cotton ball. Ike yelled when she pressed the soaked cotton to his scrape.

"I have to kill the germs so your hand won't get affected."

"You mean 'infected,' dummy," Ike said.

Leona pressed the cotton hard onto Ike's owie. He jerked his hand away.

"Sorry," she said.

"Me, too," Ike said.

Leona put two Band-Aids in an X on Ike's hand. "There. It won't get IN-fected or AF-fected," she said. "Let's go ask your mom about lunch."

It was all right with Rachel. She did notice the Band-Aids on Ike's hand and how dirty his jeans were. "Ike, be careful. You don't want to hurt your hands. No rough stuff. You have to play at the gallery next Saturday."

"What does your mom mean, you have to play at

the gallery?" Leona asked as they walked back to her house. "What are you playing at the gallery?"

"Schubert." Ike looked at Leona out of the corner of his eyes. "On the cello. What did you think I was going to play—Ping-Pong?"

Leona looked at Ike. She used one of her fixing stares on him. He didn't budge, but suddenly he blinked and began to smile. Leona burst out laughing and shoved him on the elbow. "Last one there is a rotten cucumber."

Ike was way behind Leona. Leona stood on the back step waiting for him to catch up. Instead of calling him a rotten cucumber, she said, "Time to eat."

They sat at the kitchen table and ate tacos for lunch. Leona helped Mom serve. When Rachel called to say it was time for Ike to come with her to the gallery, Ike made a face.

Leona wondered why Rachel wanted Ike to go along. Rachel was different from Mom. Mom didn't take Victoria and Albert and her wherever she went. They stayed home together sometimes. Ike didn't have anyone to be together with. Maybe that's why Rachel wanted him to go with her.

Leona talked Mom into talking Rachel into letting Ike stay the whole afternoon. "Why don't you stay with us every time your mom goes to work at the gallery?" Leona said.

"I'd like to," Ike said. "I'd like to come every day."

8

Baseball in the Park

When Ike came over the next day, Leona took him straight up to her room.

"Let's play in the box," she said. She liked to play in the box. She even wanted to share the box with Ike. Sharing with a friend was different from sharing with family. Sometimes Leona shared things with Victoria and Albert because she had to.

"I think the box would make a great spaceship," Leona said as they went up to the closet. She got down on her knees and crawled into the box. "Do you want to play planetary avengers? The planetary avengers are the good guys. They bring order to the universe."

"Hmm. Good guys?" Ike said. "Do we have to be good guys? Can't we be the bad guys? Everyone always wants the good guys to win. The bad guys never do. It isn't fair. I think the bad guys should have a chance."

"But Ike, the bad guys lose because they're the bad guys. That's how you play."

"We could take turns," Ike said. "Let's be the bad guys first."

Leona frowned at Ike. That wasn't what she had in mind. Ike prepared the ship for takeoff and began talking about how to destroy the enemy. Leona steered the ship through the galaxy and zapped the enemy. She pretended she was a good guy without telling Ike. He didn't notice.

It didn't matter anyway. Ike was playing Leona's game. Victoria and Rita never played planetary avengers with Leona. Albert did, but he goofed it up. Even if he was a bad guy, Ike was good at playing planetary avengers.

Leona could tell that Ike liked space games. He knew a lot about the solar system, especially about Mars and the moon.

"When I'm older, I plan to go to the moon," Ike told her. "I think it must be very beautiful up there with all of that thick dust. Do you want to come with me—when you're older?"

Leona liked to look at the moon, the glowing full moon with its funny-shaped shadows. Daddy said it was the face of a man, but Leona thought the shadows looked like a leaping rabbit. The moon must be awfully far away. "I'll go to the moon with you," Leona said, "if you'll go to the park and play baseball with me."

Ike grimaced as if he had swallowed a whole slice of corned beef.

Later, as Ike was leaving, Leona and Ike met Daddy in the hall. He was carrying a mug of coffee from the kitchen to his office.

"What do you think?" he said. "Isn't it about time I took a Friday off? Do you two want to go to the park with me on Friday?"

"I do. I do." Leona knew that going to the park meant baseball. She looked at Ike, wondering if he knew, too, and if he would go anyway.

"Thank you," he said to Daddy. "I'll ask Rachel. She probably won't mind."

"Yippee!" Leona shouted, and she clapped her hands.

Leona wore her Twins T-shirt to the park. Albert wore his T-ball team shirt. Ike wore a purple T-shirt with a humpback whale on it. He said he got it when he went to California with David.

"Rachel said I have to be careful not to hurt my hands," Ike said on the way to the park.

"Don't worry," Daddy said. "We'll be extra careful."

For someone who thought baseball was dumb, Ike tried really hard to learn how to bat. He didn't hit the ball every time the way Leona did. She waited for the right pitch, then *ka-wham,* she connected. She couldn't explain how she knew it was a good pitch. She just knew.

Albert was catcher behind Ike, who was batting.

Daddy stood halfway between home plate and the pitcher's mound, and Leona was on first.

"Keep your eyes on the ball," Daddy said to Ike.

Daddy pitched. The ball was inside. Ike closed his eyes, swung, and missed.

"Just jump back if the ball is too close. It won't hit you. But don't swing. Wait for a good one."

Daddy is a good teacher, Leona thought. He never makes you feel stupid when you miss. Ike missed a lot. Of course, Albert missed even more, so Ike didn't look so bad.

Finally, Ike hit the ball, and it popped over Daddy's head. Leona ran after it. "Yay, Ike! You got a hit."

Ike stood smiling. Albert shoved him and said, "Run, Ike. You've got to run to first base."

Ike trotted to the base. Leona wondered if Ike felt happy and powerful the way she did when she hit the ball. The noise of the bat thwacking the ball always made her want to celebrate.

After baseball, Daddy was in such a good mood that Leona thought it would be a good time to ask him about the tent. "Daddy, do you think you could put the tent up in the backyard?"

"Whew," Daddy said. "I'll tell you what. It's supposed to rain this weekend. I'll set it up first thing next week—that is, if you all will help me."

"We'll help," Leona said.

"I've never put up a tent before," Ike said. Leona nudged him. "But I'll help."

Daddy walked them to Ike's house and introduced himself to Rachel. She shook hands with Daddy.

"I played baseball in the park. My hands are fine," Ike said.

"Ike can hit the ball," Leona added.

"Thanks so much for taking Ike," Rachel said. "Ike and I have been talking, and we wondered if Leona could go to the opening at the gallery next Saturday. Ike is going to play the cello with a quartet there."

"Can I, Daddy, please?" Leona crossed her fingers and closed her eyes.

Daddy thought for a moment. "Thank you," he said. "I'm sure that would be fine."

On the walk home, Leona did two cartwheels in a row on the sidewalk. Then she took Daddy's hand. "Today was a great day. Thanks, Daddy."

Daddy squeezed Leona's hand, and she squeezed back.

"It was a great day because Ike went to the park with us, and he even played baseball," she told Daddy.

Ike would probably never again say that baseball was dumb, she thought. Next week would be great, too. They would set up the tent. Then Leona was going to hear Ike play the cello at an opening in Chicago. Leona wondered what an opening was. She would have to ask Ike.

9

A Real Live Artist

After breakfast on Monday morning, Leona and Ike helped Daddy set up the tent in the backyard. Then Leona and Ike moved some of the things from the box in the closet to the tent. Leona brought a sack of pretzels and some comic books. Ike ran home to get his chess set and his plastic diplodocus.

It was so hot in the tent that they left the flaps open. Ike wanted to teach Leona how to play chess, but she wanted to talk about the opening.

"I've never been to a picture opening," she said. "I went to a grand opening once, at Rossignol's hardware store. They had cookies and orange drink, and I won a candy bar. Are there prizes at a picture opening?"

"Not usually. I've been to lots of openings. People stand around and talk and look at the paintings. There's food, too, and the artist who painted the pictures is usually there."

"Wow," said Leona. "Food and a real live artist. Does the artist dress up like something? Mr. Rossignol dressed up like a squirrel at his opening and passed out popcorn."

"Artists don't dress up like squirrels," Ike said.

"Does the artist paint pictures of animals? I like skunks and raccoons the best."

"Wait until Saturday and you'll see," Ike said.

"It's hard to wait for things you want to happen."

"I know what you mean," Ike said. "I want Saturday to come, but sometimes I wish it wouldn't."

"That doesn't make sense," Leona said.

"I don't know if I'm ready."

"Oh, you mean for playing the cello. Don't worry. Victoria's piano teacher, Mrs. Swanson, always tells Victoria to close her eyes and think about the oatmeal cookies she's going to get at the reception afterwards."

"That wouldn't work for me," Ike said. "I hate oatmeal cookies."

Leona shrugged. "Then think of something you like. Think about electric trains. Think about the moon. Anyway, I'm glad I get to go."

"Me, too," Ike said. "We were lucky this time."

"What do you mean?"

"I had to talk Rachel into asking you. She was afraid I might not play as well. Actually, I have to talk her into a lot of things. Same with David. It doesn't always work. Then I have to do what they tell me to. Aren't your parents like that, too? Don't you always have to ask them first?"

"Yes," said Leona. "Daddy says that's because they have been on earth longer. He says that I can do anything I want when I'm twenty-one. I can stay up until three in the morning and eat chocolate bars for breakfast and dye my hair purple."

"Purple?" Ike groaned. "That's weird. Besides, when you are twenty-one, you won't want to dye your hair purple."

"I will too," said Leona. "And I'll wear shoes with jewels in them when I dress up, and I'm going to be a baseball player in the Major Leagues."

"Girls don't play in the Major Leagues."

"They will when I'm twenty-one," Leona argued. But she couldn't help agreeing that what Ike had said about grown-ups was true. They wouldn't both be sitting in the tent if Daddy hadn't put it up. She wouldn't be going to the gallery with Ike if Mom and Daddy had said no.

On Saturday Leona decided to wear her lavender and white polka-dot dress, her favorite, to the gallery. She was glad she had dressed up. Ike was dressed up, too. He had on a black suit and white shirt and silky black bow tie.

On the drive to Chicago Leona sat in the backseat with Ike. Ike was very quiet. Leona thought maybe he was sick. Sometimes Victoria got carsick in the backseat and had to sit in the front so she wouldn't throw up.

"What are you staring at?" Leona said.

"The air," Ike finally answered. "Don't worry. I always get this way before I play."

Leona felt like saying, "You can't stare at air. You can't see air. It's invisible." She had learned that in science last year. But she decided Ike was nervous and wouldn't be interested in science right now. "Good luck," she said.

"Thanks," said Ike and went back to staring at the air.

When they got to Chicago, Rachel hustled Leona and Ike through a small crowd of people gathered at the entrance of the gallery. Ike had to play right away. He settled down on a chair beside three men who wore black suits and bow ties, too.

Leona listened to the music. It sounded as if the volume had been turned way up. Music filled the room. While Ike played, he stared at sheets of music set on a shiny silver music stand. He looked as if he were staring at the air again.

Ike looked different, Leona thought. It was not just his clothes. His face looked different, the way he concentrated as he moved the bow across the strings of the cello. He played the way grown-ups play.

Leona felt proud of Ike. He was an important person today. So important, she worried, that after the recital Ike might not want to be her friend anymore.

When the musicians finished the piece, Leona clapped. No one else did, which Leona thought was funny. If she had played a cello in front of a crowd of people, she would have wanted them to clap.

Ike shuffled through the music on the stand. The other men were talking to one another. They were probably trying to decide what to play next.

Leona wandered off to see the paintings. Before she reached the wall where the paintings hung, she discovered a long table set with trays of food and glasses full of bubbly crystal soda pop. Leona wished it were root beer instead. Root beer was her favorite. The food looked like finger food to Leona. She grabbed four crackers spread with blackberry jam and smushed them two at a time together to make sandwiches.

Then she picked up a glass and gulped a mouthful of soda pop, which she had to spit right back into the glass. It was spoiled. She had never heard of spoiled pop before, but this was definitely spoiled. Leona didn't know what to do with the glass, so she set it back on the table. But then she thought she should stay and watch it so that no one else would take the glass of spoiled pop with her germs in it. Except, if she stood around looking at the glass, she would never see the pictures. Maybe she ought to make a sign to warn people about the glass. Or she could take the glass to the bathroom and pour the pop down the sink. But where was the bathroom?

Suddenly Leona saw Rachel. She hurried to warn her. "That glass of pop is spoiled, Mrs. Boskowitz. I tasted it. What should I do with it?"

Rachel smiled. "It's not pop, Leona. It's champagne."

"Champagne!" Leona shouted. "But that's for grown-ups."

"If you can wait, I'll give you and Ike some orange juice later." Rachel noticed Leona's crackers. "It looks as if you really like caviar."

"Oh yes," said Leona, supposing that "caviar" was a fancy word for jam and crackers. "But I like it better with peanut butter."

Carrying the crackers on her napkin, Leona walked over to a wall hung with pictures. She thought black and red and gray must be the artist's favorite colors. She stared at the first painting, then a second and third. There were shapes in these pictures, tubes and big squares. She couldn't quite figure out how the tubes and squares fit together to make something.

Studying the pictures, she bit off a piece of cracker. Whatever was on the cracker tasted sour and salty and very fishy. Right away she knew it couldn't be blackberry jam.

A man in a raincoat and a blue baseball hat stopped beside her. "Don't you like the paintings?" he said.

Leona shrugged. She couldn't talk. She couldn't open her mouth and she couldn't swallow. She held up the rest of the cracker to explain.

"Oh, of course," said the man. He took a crumpled piece of paper from his pocket. "Here, spit it out."

Leona felt relieved to be rid of the cracker. The

man took off his baseball hat. Then he wrapped
Leona's napkin around the crackers and the wadded
paper and put the napkin in his hat. He held the hat
upside down in front of him as if he expected someone
to draw a number from it.

"I'll find a trash can around here eventually," he
said. "I can't stand caviar either."

"It tastes terrible," said Leona.

The man walked around with her as she looked at
the other paintings. In one were tires and handlebars,
she was sure. "That looks like a motorcycle," said
Leona. "My uncle Rosco would like that one. He races
motorcycles."

"It is a motorcycle," the man said.

"How do you know?"

"I painted it," he said. "Sometimes I actually know
what I'm painting."

"I always know what I'm painting," Leona said. "I
mostly do skunks and raccoons."

"Good for you," said the man.

"I never met a real live artist before," Leona said.
She looked up at the man beside her. He wore thick
glasses that made his eyes look big. She wondered if
all famous artists looked like him. She thought he
should have paint on his raincoat.

"Quentin Stansfield in real live person," the man
said and held out his hand.

Leona shook hands with him. "Leona Joan Hanrahan," she said.

"Well, Leona, what do you think of the paintings?"

Leona was just going to tell the artist that she liked the paintings but she thought it must be a lot more fun to make them than to look at them. But a tall man in a black suit walked right between Leona and the artist. He waved his hands. "Masterful. You've outdone yourself this time, Quentin. Masterful."

Leona didn't like the way that man just walked in and started talking. She had been talking to the artist first, and that man just took over as if she weren't even there.

After the music stopped, Ike came running up to Leona. He carried two small bottles of orange juice and green-striped straws.

Ike shook his dark bangs out of his eyes and handed Leona a bottle of juice and a straw. He didn't look as grown-up and serious as he had when he was playing the cello with the three men. His shirt had come untucked and hung over his belt.

"Thanks, Ike." Leona took the bottle and popped a straw into it. She sipped the juice with relief. Ike hadn't forgotten her. Ike was the same skinny kid who played with her in the box. The juice tasted a thousand times better than the spoiled-pop champagne.

"Ike, you are really good at playing the cello," Leona said. "You are masterful," she added, and she meant it.

10

Victoria

That night Leona missed Victoria more than any other night since Victoria had gone to Aunt Gwendolyn's. She wanted to tell Victoria all about the gallery and Ike's recital and the real live artist she had met.

When Mom kissed her good night and said, "We're going to pick up Victoria on Tuesday night," Leona almost jumped out of bed and turned a cartwheel.

"I wish we could go now," Leona said. "Victoria's been gone forever."

But the next morning, Leona remembered out loud at breakfast, "Oh, no, I can't go to pick up Victoria. Ike and me are going to camp in the tent on Tuesday. I don't want to go to the train station. I want to get ready to camp."

"But Leona, we can't leave you home for such a long time," Mom said. "I thought you missed Victoria and that you would want to go with all of us."

"I do miss Victoria," Leona said, "at night." She didn't miss her so much during the day because then she played with Ike. "Couldn't Ike go with us?" Leona suggested. "He took me on a trip. Now it's my turn to take him on a trip."

"I suppose Ike could come," Mom said. "I'll call Rachel. Since you were planning to play together, I don't think she'll mind. You can camp out when we get back."

On Tuesday afternoon Mom, Daddy, Albert, Ike, and Leona got into the old brown station wagon. Daddy drove all the way to the train station in downtown Chicago.

Victoria's train was late, so they went to look at Lake Michigan for a while. Mom stopped to visit the Art Institute, but Leona had seen enough art at the gallery on Saturday. She and Ike and Albert went with Daddy to a computer fair. Then they met Mom for supper at a restaurant because Victoria's train still wasn't there.

Finally, the train arrived. Victoria looked different when she got off the train and came walking down the platform. Leona noticed right away. Victoria's dark hair was parted on the side and slicked back behind her ears. She wore a new shirt. It was black, with pink and silver sequins sewn in stripes across the front. Victoria looked older. Maybe she had grown older during the three weeks she stayed at Aunt Gwendolyn's.

Daddy took one of Victoria's suitcases and hugged her. Then Mom hugged her and Albert grabbed her hand. Finally, Leona had a chance to say something.

She gave Victoria a quick hug and said, "I missed you, Victoria."

"Me, too," said Victoria.

Leona tugged at Ike's jacket sleeve to make him come closer. "This is my friend Ike. He moved into the duplex down the street while you were gone. You should hear Ike play the cello. He played at a grand opening at his mom's art gallery. And his grandfather was a famous president."

"Hi, Ike," Victoria said. "It looks like I missed something when I was gone."

"Nice to meet you, Victoria," Ike said. "Actually I'm just named after a famous president. He wasn't my grandfather."

Everyone helped Victoria carry her suitcases and two bulging shopping bags from L. S. Ayres. Everyone except Mom and Albert. Albert always managed to fall asleep when they had to walk far or carry things. Mom pushed him in a baggage cart.

"Guess what," Leona said to Victoria as they got into the station wagon. "Ike is staying all night. We're going to sleep out in the tent."

"That's nice," Victoria said. She settled down in the car seat with a sigh. "Aunt Gwendolyn's neighbors are really nice," she said. "They have a girl your age, Leona, and a boy named Jason. Jason is fourteen. We all went to the summer festival together. It was great. Fireworks and rock music. We stayed out past midnight."

"Midnight!" Leona shouted. "Are you going to tell Mom?"

Victoria shrugged her shoulders.

"I don't care much for rock music," Ike said suddenly.

Leona had almost forgotten he was there. Maybe Ike was feeling left out. "I don't like rock music either," she said.

"Since when?" Victoria said. Then she waved her hand. "So what? Do you want to hear what else we did? We went to a big department store called L. S. Ayres. And we went to the movies and saw a double feature. They were both PG-13. Aunt Gwendolyn took me to her health club, too. I know how to play racquetball and I'm good at tennis. Aunt Gwendolyn said so."

"Do they play baseball at a health club?" Leona asked.

Ike spoke before Victoria could answer. "No baseball. David goes to a health club, and they don't have baseball."

"Who's David?" Victoria said, sounding annoyed.

"David is Ike's dad. His parents are divorced," Leona said.

"Oh," said Victoria.

Albert popped up from the front seat. "Mom and Daddy aren't going to be divorced."

"We know, Albert. We know," Leona said.

Victoria looked puzzled. "What did he say that for?"

Ike looked at Leona. "Albert just has an active imagination."

"That means he says things that aren't true," Leona said.

The rest of the way home, Leona and Ike listened to Victoria talk about shopping and rock music and Jason and which hair spray holds hair in place the best but doesn't destroy the ozone layer and Aunt Gwendolyn's compact disc player and Jason and how Victoria was invited back next summer and Jason was going to write her letters. Leona could feel something different about Victoria, besides her new hairstyle.

"I'm hungry!" Albert shouted as they pulled into the driveway.

"It's late," Mom said.

"It's only eleven," Victoria said.

"If you all get ready for bed right away, I'll make you some of my famous popcorn," Daddy said.

"That sounds like a bribe," Ike whispered to Leona.

"You should taste Daddy's popcorn. It's the best in the world."

As soon as they were dressed for bed, Mom served them buttery popcorn at the kitchen table.

"Can Ike and me take our popcorn to the tent?"

"Sorry. This popcorn is swimming in butter," Mom said. "It will be too messy."

"I want to go in the tent, too," Albert said.

"There isn't enough room," Mom said. "Come on, I'll tell you a story and tuck you in bed."

"I'll say good night to you now, Leona." She hugged Leona and gave her a kiss on the forehead. She kissed Ike, too, on his dark hair that drooped over his forehead. "Good night. Don't stay up talking too long."

"We won't."

"Thanks, Leona, for letting me have the room to myself tonight," Victoria said. "At Aunt Gwendolyn's I had a room of my own."

"That's okay," Leona said. She would rather sleep in the tent anyway.

"Go on, you two," said Daddy. "I'll clean up. Don't let the bears in."

"There aren't any bears in Winnetka," Leona said. She turned to Ike. "There's nothing to be afraid of in the backyard."

11

"The Black Cat"

It was dark outside. Leona looked up at the sky and saw that the moon had gotten lost in thick gray clouds. She beamed her flashlight on the ground and led the way to the tent.

As soon as she and Ike were settled, Leona asked, "Want to play Fish?"

"I prefer to read," Ike said. "I always read before I go to bed. Do you have any books in the tent?"

Leona fumbled through the pile of objects at the back of the tent. *"Baseball's Greatest Hitters,"* she read from a paperback book she found. "Or comic books." She tossed a comic book to Ike.

Ike dropped the comic. "Don't you have *The Iliad* and *The Odyssey?* I've been reading *The Iliad.* I don't usually read comics or books for kids."

"Mom and Daddy have some thick books in the fireplace room," Leona said. "I can go see."

Leona grabbed the flashlight and crawled out of the tent. Ike followed her.

"You don't have to come."

"You have the flashlight," Ike said.

At the back door, Leona put her finger to her lips. "Don't make any noise," she whispered.

Leona led the way through the kitchen to the hallway and tiptoed down the hall to the fireplace room. When they were in the room, she closed the door and turned the light on.

War and Peace, The Good Earth, Barefoot Boy with Cheek, World Enough and Time. There was nothing about an ill lad, no story about an odd sea.

Ike studied the bookshelves. He ran his fingers down one book at a time. Leona stared at the shelves, looking for the biggest book she could find. Then she saw it, a thick black book with a green label. *The Stories of Edgar Allan Poe.* She took the book down, opened it, and looked at some of the titles. "This is perfect," Leona said, when she saw a title with long words she didn't recognize. Maybe Ike wouldn't know all the words either.

"Edgar Allan Poe. I've heard of him," Ike said when she showed him the book.

In the tent Ike settled down with the big book.

Leona opened an Archie comic book. Ike announced, "I think I'll read 'The Black Cat.' "

"That sounds like an easy story," Leona said.

It was quiet in the tent except for the swift rustle of pages turning. Leona turned four or five pages in the time it took Ike to turn one.

"Oh. Ugh!" Ike said suddenly.

"What's wrong?" Leona said.

"The man telling the story. Do you know what he did to his black cat? He took a knife—"

"I don't want to know," Leona interrupted. "I don't like people who are mean to cats."

"It's not all his fault," Ike said. "It's because of the wine. He drank so much wine that he came home and hurt his cat."

"You mean that drinking wine will make you mean to cats?" Leona thought about the champagne at the gallery opening. "Is champagne like wine?"

"I think so," Ike said.

"Then I'm so glad it tasted terrible and I spit it out. I couldn't stand to be mean to cats. Why don't you read another story?" Leona suggested.

"No. I want to see if the cat gets even."

"Well, read it to yourself." Leona looked down at her comic book, but she was thinking about the poor black cat. Then she began to listen to the night noises outside the tent. Crickets, she reasoned, when she heard the buzz and chirp and throb. Or locusts. But there were noises she wasn't sure about. A door slamming? Wind blowing through the leaves?

"He killed the cat," Ike whispered suddenly, and Leona jumped.

As Ike started to read out loud, Leona reached for the book. "No, Ike."

Ike pulled the book toward his chest. "Let me

finish. I think the cat is going to come back as a ghost."

Leona grabbed the flashlight. "I'll turn the light out if you read out loud again. And don't tell me how the story ends." Leona knew it was one of those stories that didn't have a happy ending. She liked happy endings.

Ike shrugged his shoulders and began reading silently. Leona put the flashlight back. She didn't even look at the comic on her lap. Instead, she wondered about ghosts and cats. Could there be such a thing as a cat ghost? What would a cat ghost look like? Would it be mean? The cat ghost in Ike's story would be mean. It would want to get even. It would come back at night probably and creep up and—

Leona thought she heard a faint cry. Was it coming from the front yard? The cry sounded louder.

Ike looked up. "What's that?"

"Crickets." Leona's throat felt tight. Her voice came out squeaky.

"Are you sure?"

"Sure. I hear crickets all the time," Leona said to convince herself. She wondered if Ike had heard that strange, whining cry in the yard. The pounding in her ears made it hard for her to hear even the crickets. Had the crickets stopped? Maybe something had scared them, something that was coming closer and closer to the tent.

Leona stared at Ike as she strained to listen. He stared back, and Leona knew he had heard it, too.

Suddenly the bushes rustled behind the tent.

"*Eeeowwww. Eeeowwww. Pfffft!*" shrieked through the night.

Leona jumped to her knees and crawled out of the tent. She got up and ran as fast as she could. She could feel the ghost of a black cat chasing her. She bumped into the back door and the demon fell against her.

"Ouch."

"Ouch to you," said Ike. "Let's get inside."

Leona opened the door and they both slipped into the safety of the house and collapsed on the kitchen chairs. Leona could feel her heart thumping. She felt sweaty and a little dizzy. When she got her breath back, she stood up and turned on the light over the sink. She looked at Ike. He was so pale that his eyes seemed to jump out of his face. He looked like he needed pepping up.

"Do you want some ginger ale?" Leona said.

"Yes, please," Ike said and sighed.

Leona poured two glasses full of ginger ale and took some carrot sticks out of the refrigerator. Crunching on a carrot made the world seem more real to her.

"It was a cat fight," she said, feeling safer and much braver in the kitchen. "Cat fights sound horrible. I've heard them before from my window upstairs."

"I wouldn't want to have a cat that fights," Ike said.

Leona thought Ike might not want to go back outside to the tent tonight. Although she didn't say so to Ike, she had no intention of going back outside herself.

When they finished eating, Leona unrolled Albert's napping quilt on the floor in the playroom.

When Leona woke, Ike wasn't there. He wasn't in the kitchen either. Leona went to look for him.

"Where's Ike?" Leona asked Mom, who was carrying a laundry basket up from the basement.

"Oh, good morning, Leona. Ike's mom called at eight. Ike had to go home in a hurry. His dad is taking him someplace today."

"But Mom, why didn't you wake me up?"

"You seemed so tired. I let you sleep late."

"I didn't want to sleep late." Leona ran upstairs to her room. She jerked her drawer so hard that it fell on the floor with a boom. Victoria moaned and put a pillow over her head. Leona had forgotten that Victoria was back home. The drawer was too heavy to put back. She took out her clothes and tried to dress quietly.

She kept thinking about Ike. Maybe Ike hadn't left with his dad yet. Or maybe he was already back. Ike hadn't said that his dad was coming today. His dad always came on Saturday or Sunday. Leona wondered what was going on.

She hurried to Ike's.

"Is Ike home?" she asked Rachel.

"Not right now." Rachel held the front door open and spoke as softly as an usher at the door of the church on Sunday. "He's with his father. We didn't expect his father." Then she added, "Something came up."

"When will Ike be back?"

"I don't know. If it's not too late, I'll have him call you."

"Have him call me anyway," Leona said.

Leona went to the backyard to check the tent. The door flap was draped across the side of the tent. It looked quiet and cozy and perfectly safe. Leona crawled inside and sat down for a minute. There was nothing scary about the tent this morning. She and Ike should have stayed in the tent last night.

Leona picked up the flashlight. She shifted the switch off and on, but nothing happened. Of course, the batteries were worn out. They had left it on all night. The thick black book was lying open on the tent floor where Ike had dropped it. Leona read the last three paragraphs of "The Black Cat."

"Weird," she said and closed the book. She had known it wouldn't have a happy ending.

12

Hurricane Ike

Leona stared at the band of light on the ceiling. The light came from the hall and shone through the open door of her room. Tonight she was back in the top bunk. She hadn't seen the ceiling for a long time. It looked new and different to her.

"Are you asleep, Leona?" Victoria whispered from the bottom bunk.

"No." Leona was trying to stay awake in case Ike called. He hadn't called back today. Leona expected him to call, even if it was late.

"If you tell me about Ike, I'll tell you about Jason," Victoria said.

Leona didn't know how Victoria could say anything more about Jason. She had talked about him all day. Leona knew more about Jason than she knew about anyone else she had never met before. She knew he was going to high school next year and that he was tall. He played basketball, and because he was so good he was going to play on the varsity team. He liked butterscotch sundaes and he didn't like to dance. What else could Victoria tell her?

Leona knew that she would listen anyway. She liked whispering at night. It was what she had missed most when Victoria was at Aunt Gwendolyn's.

"Leona, I'm waiting," Victoria said. "So tell me about Ike. He seems sort of—different."

"Different?" Leona said. "Maybe. He's smart. He reads thick books with sad endings, but he's not good at climbing trees. He has to be careful all the time not to hurt his hands because he's a great cello player."

"You mean, he's going to be a great cellist."

"No, I mean he's a great cello player now."

"I can climb trees," Victoria said. "I play the piano, and I don't have to worry about hurting my hands."

"It's not the same," Leona said.

"Oh. Well." Victoria didn't seem interested in finding out why. Leona heard her sigh. "I wish I could have stayed longer at Aunt Gwendolyn's. I wish you had come, too, Leona. You could have made friends with Jason's sister."

"I made friends with Ike."

"You could have made friends with Ike when you came home," Victoria said.

Leona didn't think so. If she had gone with Victoria, then she would have come home and played with Victoria, as usual. And if Victoria hadn't gone to Aunt Gwendolyn's, Leona would have been too busy with her and Rita to make friends with Ike. Leona was too sleepy to explain all of this tonight. She began to think about the things that wouldn't have happened if Victoria hadn't gone to Aunt Gwendolyn's. For one thing, Leona wouldn't be listening to Victoria whisper about how Jason was going to write her a letter this week. Leona tried hard to keep her eyes open while she listened, but she fell asleep.

The next morning Leona phoned Ike. The line was busy. She hung up the phone and went out the front door.

Victoria was sitting on the top porch step. "I'm tired of waiting," she said. "I don't think the mail's ever going to come."

"I'm tired of waiting, too. I'm going over to Ike's. See you later." Leona trotted down the sidewalk and hopped up the three steps to Ike's front door. She rang the doorbell.

"Hi, Ike. Do you want to play at my house?" she asked when Ike opened the door.

Ike shrugged his shoulders. "I don't feel like it."

"Do you want to play here?" Leona wondered if Ike's dad had brought his train set. Maybe he had, and Ike hadn't finished putting it together yet, so he didn't want to show it to Leona. Sometimes Leona felt like that. When she got a puzzle at Christmas, she wanted to put it together by herself before she showed anyone.

"Did your dad bring your train set?"

"Train set?" Ike said. "No. He didn't bring anything. We went out for lunch." Ike chewed on his lower
lip.

"I hope he brings it soon," Leona said. "He probably told you he is too busy. That's what Mom and
Daddy always say."

"He's not too busy. He told me that he just quit his
job and took another one so he would have more time."
Ike turned and stomped upstairs.

Leona hesitated at the bottom of the stairway.
Maybe Ike wants to be alone, she thought.

"Leona, come on," Ike shouted.

Leona wasn't sure if she should go up. She wondered why Ike was acting funny. It probably had something to do with what came up yesterday. Or maybe
Ike was kidding about the train set. Maybe he had set
it up in his room and was going to surprise her.

Leona climbed the stairs and went into Ike's room.
If there was a train set, she couldn't see it. The room
was a mess. Toys, games, books, and puzzles were all
over the room. A Monopoly board lay unfolded on the
bed and tiny black chess figures littered the floor.

"What happened?" Leona said. "Sometimes Victoria and I make a mess, but it's never this bad. Your
mom is going to be mad."

"She knows," Ike said. "I don't care." He fidgeted
with a piece of notebook paper he had folded like an
accordion. Ike reminded Leona of Mitchell Reed when

Mitchell got in trouble for pulling Leona's hair at school. Mitchell always looked mad for getting caught but happy that he had done it.

Then Leona saw the suitcase, the one that was always closed up tight, ready for Ike to take when he went to visit his father. It lay wide open, propped against the wall. Shirts, pajamas, socks, robe, and underwear were scattered across the floor. The clothes looked as if they had been hanging on a clothesline and a storm had come up and blown them off.

"It looks like a hurricane hit your room," Leona said. "Hurricane Ike. Is this why you can't go outside and play?"

Ike nodded. "But it's not my fault. Actually it's David's fault and Rachel's fault."

"Did they have a fight in your room?"

"Not exactly," Ike said. "But they argued a lot. And then they decided that I am supposed to go live with David before school starts."

"What?" Leona shouted. "What do you mean?"

"David wants to send me to a special school. It's near where he lives. That's what they argued about. Rachel said no, and David said she was being unreasonable. They didn't ask me what I thought. Then David and I came back from the restaurant, and they sort of decided. Before school starts, I have to go live with David.

"Rachel says it will be good for David to have to be

responsible for a child for twenty-four hours a day. Anyway, Rachel's planning to go on a trip then." He stopped and swallowed. "Why do they have to decide? Why can't I be responsible for myself?"

Ike kicked the pillow on the floor at his feet. Then suddenly he picked it up and threw it at Leona. "I'm not moving."

Leona was too surprised to duck. The pillow bumped against her arm and fell to the floor. She grabbed it and swung it back over her shoulder. "You can't move. You're my best friend," she shouted and threw the pillow back toward Ike.

The pillow sailed into the curtain, then flopped onto Ike's head. He clutched the pillow and ran over to clobber Leona. She reached for a large stuffed tiger. Holding the tiger by the tail, she swung it into Ike's pillow.

Ike charged and bashed the tiger. "Take that."

"And that," Leona shouted back. They jumped on the bed, shouting at each other. They bashed the tiger and the pillow together again and again. Finally, Leona whacked Ike on the shoulder with the tiger. Ike doubled up over his pillow and started laughing.

Leona laughed, too. She laughed so hard that she sat down on the tiger to get her breath. For a minute she forgot she was at Ike's house. She thought she was at her own house and that Daddy would come in the room and say, "Calm down, now. The fun is over." He always did that when she and Victoria and Albert had pillow fights. Then they had to pick everything up and make the bed or smooth the wrinkles out of the cover.

"Get off the bed," Leona said.

"Why?"

"So I can make it." Leona slid off the bed. "You always make the bed and pick up after a pillow fight."

"I never had a pillow fight before," Ike said.

"Maybe not, but you sure made a mess." Leona could understand about the mess. She thought she understood why Ike had gotten mad. But she knew he would feel better if he cleaned up.

Leona crouched on the floor and began to pick up chess figures. Ike didn't argue. He got the wooden chess box from under the bed and helped.

"You really make a lot of noise when you pick up," Rachel said, standing in the doorway.

"We just jumped up and down a little before we got started," Leona said.

"Thanks for helping, Leona," Rachel said. "You are such a good friend to Ike." She turned and went back downstairs.

Leona and Ike arranged the books and games on the shelves.

"Am I really your best friend?" Ike asked.

"I said so, didn't I?" It had felt right when Leona had said it. Even if Ike wasn't the best friend she had imagined for herself, Ike was special. She liked to be with him. If Ike moved, it wouldn't be the same. Maybe Ike's mom and dad would change their minds. Grown-ups change their minds a lot. And they say things they don't mean when they're mad, Leona knew.

Leona worried as she walked home for lunch. What if Ike's parents didn't change their minds? What if Ike did have to leave? Leona would lose her best friend in the neighborhood.

Even worse than worrying was the feeling that there was nothing she could do.

13

The Moon
in the Closet

In the afternoon Ike came over and played checkers
in the tent with Leona. The top of the tent sagged in
the middle. Leona kept bumping it when she moved
to get a better view of the checkerboard.

It was hard to concentrate. Leona knew Ike was
thinking about what it would be like if he went to live
with his dad. She was, too, but she wanted to think
about something else.

"Let's go climb the tree," Leona said.

"What?"

"The tree. Let's climb the tree." Leona scuttled out
of the tent and ran to the maple tree. Pulling herself
up on the swing rope made her feel better. She stepped
onto a branch and climbed up as high as she could go.

She looked down. Ike grunted as he struggled up
the rope. When he reached the branch, he began to
climb rapidly.

"Be careful, Ike." Leona said. "You're going to
scrape your hands."

"I don't care," Ike said. He sat on the branch below her.

Leona looked out across the backyards. "Look, Ike. If you stretch up, you can see the park."

"I can see it," Ike said, craning his neck. "This is a neat spot. I like it up here." Ike had never climbed up so high.

"Me, too," said Leona.

"I like the tent, too," he added. "And I really like the box in the closet."

"Me, too," Leona said. "And you know what I think? I think that since you like it here, you ought to stay with us, instead of moving." Leona couldn't help talking about the move, even if she had climbed up the tree in order not to think about it. "I could ask Mom and Daddy."

"They wouldn't let me live here."

"They might," Leona hoped out loud. "They like you. Albert likes you. Victoria will, too, when she gets to know you better. I'll wait until Mom and Daddy are in a good mood, and then I'll ask them."

"I hope they're in a good mood soon," Ike said.

That night at supper, Daddy was talking about a "very interesting phone call" he had had in the afternoon. "I think it's a breakthrough," he said, and whenever he said "breakthrough," it was a good sign.

They had spaghetti, everyone's favorite. Victoria

said to Mom, "Your spaghetti sauce is better than Aunt Gwendolyn's," and Mom looked happy.

Leona decided it was a good time to talk about Ike. "Why does Ike have to move?" she asked. "He doesn't want to go away."

"I miss Ike," Albert said.

"He isn't gone yet," Leona said.

"Ike isn't here," Albert said. "I miss Ike."

"I think we are all going to miss Ike," Mom said.

Daddy started talking in his serious voice. "Leona, I'm afraid that lots of things happen that we don't want to happen. Sometimes changes can work out for the best."

"I don't think it's going to work out at all," Leona said. "I wish I could talk to Ike's dad. I would tell him that Ike is happy here and that my school is just fine and Ike can play the cello every day if he wants to. Or maybe you should talk to Ike's mom and dad. Grownups listen better to other grown-ups. Tell them that Ike should live here."

"Well," Mom said, "I did talk with Rachel today. She is worried. She doesn't know if she is doing the right thing, but she thinks it will be good for David to take care of Ike and for them to be together."

That's not what Leona had wanted Mom to say. "But Ike told me he likes to be here, at our house. He's happy when he's with us."

"That's good, Leona. I'm glad he likes to be with

us, but he does belong with his parents." Mom shook her head and smiled. "Leona, do you remember the day Ike moved? You stormed into the kitchen and told me you hated him."

Leona could remember the day Mom was talking about, but she couldn't remember how she had felt. She couldn't remember hating Ike. "I don't hate Ike. He is my best friend."

"People can change," Daddy said. "They can change from hating to loving and from loving to hating."

"That's the truth," Victoria said with conviction.

"But why do people change in the first place?" Leona said. "And why can't they change back?"

Mom and Daddy didn't have an answer. They hadn't said that Ike could come live with them either.

The next day Ike asked Leona, "What did your parents say?"

Leona hesitated. "Well . . ."

"Didn't you ask them?" Ike said.

"Sort of." Leona didn't want to disappoint Ike by telling him her parents didn't say he could live with them. But she couldn't lie to Ike. Ike was her friend. "They didn't say you could," she admitted, "not yet. I'm going to keep asking until they do."

Every day Leona asked Mom, but Mom always said the same thing: "Ike belongs with his parents."

Finally, Leona pleaded with Mom right in front of Ike. "Please, Mom, let Ike stay here with us." Victoria always asked Mom about sleepovers with Rita right in front of Rita. Then Mom said yes because she didn't want to hurt Rita's feelings. But it didn't work for Leona.

"I'm sorry," Mom said. "Ike can't live with us. But he can come and visit."

"Good," said Leona. "Then can he visit now?"

Mom smiled and shook her head. "I think you know I didn't mean now. Not yet."

"Come on, Ike." Leona made her voice sound as miserable as she could. "It's probably the last time we'll be able to play planetary avengers."

They went up to the closet and prepared the box for takeoff.

"The moon?" Leona asked.

Ike sat at the controls beside Leona. He nodded. "I wish I could go to the moon, the real moon, instead of David's house."

"Ike." Leona frowned. "We have to concentrate." It was hard to play planetary avengers if you thought about something else.

Ike pushed buttons, Leona pushed buttons, and they took off for the moon.

"We are approaching the moon," Ike said after a minute. "Prepare for landing."

Leona looked out the window flap they had cut in

the box. The closet light was turned off. The flashlight in the box sent a faint streak of light into the closet. The rest was dark and quiet. Leona imagined that it was dark and quiet on the real moon, too. Dark and quiet and far away, just the way it was in the closet right now. Leona thought about what Ike had said about going to the moon. She thought about the spaceship and the moon and the box and the closet.

"Ike, this is the moon!" she shouted. Her voice echoed in the box. "This is the moon you can come to."

"I know," Ike said. "We're going to sink into fifteen feet of lunar dust if you don't get the landing gear out."

"Ike, I'm not playing anymore—"

"Aw, Leona, come on." Ike sounded disappointed.

"Listen, Ike. You don't have to go to the real moon. You don't have to go with your dad. You can come to the moon here in the closet. You can come to the box."

"You mean, hide in the box?" Leona knew from Ike's voice that he wasn't playing anymore either.

"Just for a while," she said. "Until my parents say you can stay." Leona knew that when her parents saw how happy Ike was with them, they would let him stay.

Ike grinned. "It's a great idea."

"You'll have to be quiet, Ike. You won't be able to come out until everyone is in bed. I can bring you snacks. Except," Leona worried out loud, "Victoria spends a lot of time in our room. She's always reading or talking to Rita on the phone. Maybe I should tell Victoria right away."

Ike shook his head. "We have to plan it by ourselves. Don't tell anyone."

Leona nodded. Ike was right. She wouldn't tell. Victoria had told her everything she knew about Jason, but Jason wasn't going to hide in the closet. Ike was. Maybe there are secrets you have with your best friend that you can't even tell your sister.

Leona and Ike stayed in the box. Instead of playing planetary avengers, they made secret plans.

14

The Secret
in the Box

Leona knew that Ike couldn't play the day before he
was supposed to move. He was too busy running er-
rands with Rachel and packing. But for their plan to
work, he would have to sneak over to Leona's before
his dad came. Tomorrow he was supposed to come
over to say goodbye.

Leona was not very good at waiting. She didn't want
to talk to anyone either. She was afraid she would say
something about their plan.

For a while she sat in the tent. Then she climbed
the maple tree. After lunch she went up to her room.

"Can't I have any privacy?" Victoria said. "I want
to be alone."

"I want to be alone, too," Leona said.

"We can't be alone together."

"Then you stay on the bed. I'll go someplace private." Leona went to the closet and crawled into her
secret box. She beamed the flashlight on her book and
read *Baseball's Greatest Hitters* for the one thousandth

time. Then she went through her baseball cards, one by one. She arranged them according to the alphabet, first by their last names, then by their first names. After that she arranged them according to which hand they batted with, then which hand they threw with. Finally, she put them in order with her favorite one first and so on. It was a long afternoon.

The night was even longer. Leona lay awake on the top bunk. She fiddled with her sheet and finally kicked it off. She hugged her skunk puppet and pulled at the fuzz of its tail. Leaning over the edge of the bunk, she stared down at Victoria, who was sleeping soundly.

Then Leona heard a noise and sat straight up. It was a weird howling sound. Another cat fight, she thought. She climbed down from bed to close the window so the cats wouldn't wake Victoria. She hoped no one else in her family would wake up either.

From the window she looked down at the front walk. It glowed white in the moonlight.

"*Rrrrow. Rrrrow. Fffft. Rrrrrow,*" came from the bushes. She waited for two cats to jump out and tear at each other. The bushes shook. Someone kid-sized stepped onto the walk and cupped his hands over his mouth. "*Rrrow. Rrrow. Fffft. Rrrrow.*"

"Ike!" Leona muffled her shout with her hand. Then she hurried downstairs and unlocked the front door.

"Ike!" she whisper-yelled from the porch.

Ike dragged his suitcase from the bushes. Leona waved to him to come to the porch. She felt a little dizzy, as if she were tipping over the edge of a Ferris wheel seat to look at the ground below.

Ike reached the porch and Leona grabbed the suitcase to keep from shaking. "Come on," she said as they went in the front door. "And keep quiet."

Carrying the suitcase, Leona led Ike up the stairs to her room. She could hear him breathing as if he had just run a race. They walked on tiptoes, but the floor creaked beneath their footsteps.

Once they were both in the closet, Leona closed the door and eased to the floor. She crawled into the box to fetch the flashlight. She brought it out and turned it on so they could see. They were afraid to talk, so they made faces at each other and talked with their hands.

Leona took the suitcase to the back of the closet and stuffed it behind the long dresses Mom kept there. She handed Ike the flashlight and pointed to the box. Ike crawled in and turned around. He held the flashlight under his chin and made a face. Leona clapped her hand over her mouth to muffle a laugh. She waved to Ike and put her head on the palm of her hand, closing her eyes to show him he ought to go to sleep. Ike nodded and waved.

Leona concentrated on being quiet as she climbed back into the top bunk. It was impossible for her to

sleep. Victoria murmured and turned over again and again. Leona was sure she heard noises coming from the box. She was afraid everyone else in the house would hear.

And what about tomorrow? She thought about all the things she would have to do to make sure no one found Ike. First, she would make a sign—TOP SECRET— and tape it on the box. She could turn the box around, scrunch it against the wall, and put the sign on the back.

When would she be able to talk to Ike? Maybe they could talk when Victoria went downstairs for breakfast or when she was in the bathroom.

And what would she say to Ike's mom and dad if they asked her about Ike? What would she say to Mom and Daddy? Leona was not good at lying. She had never really lied about anything big before. Even when she told a little fib, Mom always knew.

Albert was a problem, too. Leona would have to make sure to watch out for him. He might run into her closet for some crazy reason. Albert did things like that.

Leona heard a noise in the room and forgot tomorrow's problems. She listened with a scary feeling that someone was sneaking up on her. Something popped up over the back of the bed. "Pssst," it whispered. Leona almost screamed. Then she saw it was Ike. She closed her eyes and blew out a lungful of air.

"I've got to go to the bathroom," Ike whispered.

Leona pointed to the door and followed Ike down the back of the bed. She didn't want to take any chances. She showed him where the upstairs bathroom was.

"Don't flush," she said and waited in the hall.

Leona felt safer in the hall. On the way back to the room she whispered, "Is it okay in the box?"

"Fine," Ike said. "I just can't fall asleep."

Leona nodded. They went back to her room. Ike sneaked to the closet. Leona climbed into bed and began to worry again. Finally, she fell asleep.

"Aw, Mom. It's too early," Leona heard Victoria complain. Then she felt Mom's hand squeeze her shoulder. "Leona, time for breakfast. You want to be ready when Ike comes."

Leona gasped. "Ike!" She sat up suddenly. She rubbed her eyes and blinked. It came back to her. Ike was not coming this morning. Ike was already here. Ike was in the box in the closet.

Mom stepped back, looking up at Leona. "You do remember? Ike is leaving today."

"Oh, yes. I remember. I really remember," Leona said. She scrambled down the ladder. "Victoria, rise and shine," she said loudly. Then she turned toward the closet door. "Let's go *downstairs* and have *breakfast*. How about *pancakes*, Mom?" Leona said. Mom nodded and smiled.

Victoria propped herself up on one elbow and

opened her eyes. "I'll be right down." She yawned as Mom left the room.

"Hurry, Victoria. Hurry up!" Leona pulled Victoria's arm. "First we go to the bathroom, then we go eat breakfast. After breakfast—"

"Leona, who do you think you are—Mary Poppins?" Victoria slowly emerged from bed, stood up, and stretched.

"Albert," Leona said. "I've got to wake him up." She added as an excuse, "Albert loves *pancakes.*"

Albert was not in his bed. Leona headed downstairs. She froze when she saw Albert throw open the front door. He stood listening for a moment, then shouted, "Mo-om, Ike's dad is at the door!"

15

Staring at Air

Leona sat down on the stairs. Hiding behind the banister, she watched the front doorway.

Mom came running. She waved for Mr. Boskowitz to come in.

Mr. Boskowitz was all dressed up. He had on a gray suit and a red tie. He had dark brown hair like Ike. He looked a lot like Ike, only he was taller.

Leona saw him reach out to shake hands with Mom. Mom wiped her hand on her sweatshirt and shook hands.

Mr. Boskowitz looked down and coughed. When he spoke, his voice was so quiet Leona couldn't hear what he was saying.

She could hear Mom. "Gone!" Mom shouted, shaking her head. Then she said something about being sure they would find Ike soon, and everything would be all right.

Leona thought that everything would be all right if they didn't find Ike, not yet. Ike had to stay in the box for now.

Mom led Mr. Boskowitz toward the living room. "I'll call Leona."

Leona turned to run back to her room and crashed into Victoria, who was sleepily coming down the stairs.

"Watch out," Victoria snapped. "Who was at the door? I heard someone talking."

"Ike's dad. He went in the living room with Mom."

"Where's Ike? I thought he was coming over today."

"Ike's gone," Leona said weakly.

"Leona," Mom called. "Hurry downstairs. Ike's dad is here to talk to you."

Leona followed Victoria down the stairs. Mom's voice sounded so serious that even Albert left the cartoons he was watching on TV to come to the living room.

Mr. Boskowitz was sitting on the sofa. "This is Mr. Boskowitz, Ike's dad," Mom said.

"I know," Albert said. "I opened the door."

"Shhh," Leona hissed. She felt so nervous she had to say something, make some kind of noise.

"Ike isn't at home. His parents are very worried. They thought, Leona, that Ike might have told you something."

Mr. Boskowitz stood up and walked over to Leona. He looked very serious. He looked sad, too.

"Leona, did Ike say anything to you about running away?"

Leona tried to think clearly. Running away? No, Ike had talked about hiding. They had both talked about hiding, not running away. Mr. Boskowitz was asking about running away. Leona's stomach felt twisted. Her voice came out squeaky. "No, Ike never talked about running away."

"Maybe you talked about it to Ike, Leona. And then he got ideas from you," Victoria said. She turned to explain to Mr. Boskowitz. "Leona almost ran away last year."

"But Victoria, I didn't run away. I changed my mind. Remember?" Leona said. "I didn't give Ike ideas."

"Ike is not easily influenced," Mr. Boskowitz said. Then he murmured as if he were talking to himself, "Ike is a sensitive boy. He is also very bright and talented. He might be difficult sometimes. Rachel says so, but I like being with him. I—I don't know what I would do—"

Oh, no. Leona was afraid Mr. Boskowitz was going to cry. If he did, she would probably tell him where Ike was. She wished he would leave.

"I'm sure he's around," Mom said.

"Maybe he's at Ralph's house," Leona said.

"Ike doesn't play with Ralph," Albert said.

Leona nudged Albert with her elbow. Then she looked down at the floor so she wouldn't have to look at Mr. Boskowitz's sad brown eyes.

Mr. Boskowitz touched Leona on the shoulder. "If you can think of anyplace he might be, or remember anything he said, please tell me."

Leona noticed a black dot of fingernail polish on her big toe. It looked strange. She wished she could wipe it away right now.

She nodded and looked up. "I will," she said.

"Mr. Boskowitz, would you like a cup of coffee?" Mom asked.

"Thank you. No. I must get back to Rachel. Someone may have called. Rachel is a bit of a wreck."

"We'll do all we can," Mom said and went with Mr. Boskowitz to the front door.

"What a weird thing to do," Victoria said. "Ike just disappears before he is supposed to leave with his dad. Why doesn't he want to live with his dad, anyway? His dad seems nice."

"I don't know. Maybe he is just acting nice and he is really mean," Leona said, but she didn't think it was true. "Maybe Ike likes to be here."

"But he isn't here, Leona. He's gone."

Leona felt her face get hot. "I didn't mean here. I meant this neighborhood." She lagged behind as Victoria headed toward the kitchen. Mom met them in the hall. She looked worried. "Victoria, could you and Leona make the pancakes? Go ahead, Albert, you help, too. I'm going to tell Daddy, then phone Ralph's mom and Mrs. Montgomery to let them know."

Leona shrugged. She turned to follow Victoria to the kitchen but stopped suddenly when she saw Ike at the top of the stairs. She watched Ike disappear in an instant. Then Albert ran right into her.

"Gosh, Albert. You should watch where you're going," she said. She didn't think that Albert had seen Ike. But what was Ike doing out of the box? Had he seen his dad? Had he been listening? How did he feel after he saw how worried his dad was? Leona wasn't sure how she felt, herself. She wished that Mr. Boskowitz hadn't come.

Leona herded Albert into the kitchen. She wanted to keep an eye on him while she and Victoria made breakfast. Leona watched tiny bubbles pop up on the pancake batter in the skillet. The bubbles glistened for a moment, then burst into craters. Leona wished the pancakes would cook faster. She wanted breakfast to be over so she could go back upstairs.

Using two skillets, Leona and Victoria cooked a dozen pancakes and served them—four apiece—at the kitchen table. Albert passed the syrup around after using it first.

Before Leona poured syrup on her pancakes, she slipped two cakes from her plate and set them on her lap. The pancakes were uncomfortably warm. She moved them onto the chair seat beside her, then drowned the pancakes on her plate in syrup and gobbled them down.

"Leona, you eat too fast," Victoria complained.

"I eat fast, too," Albert said. He pushed his syrupy plate away from him. There were no pancakes left. He jumped down from his chair.

"Albert," Victoria ordered, "you are so sticky, you'd better wash your hands before you touch anything."

He ran down the hall.

Leona stuck the pancakes under the waistband of her pajama bottoms.

"You're worried, aren't you?" Victoria said. "I can tell. You're acting so upset. Don't worry. They'll find Ike. I read in a magazine that if you start looking right away, you have a better chance of finding a missing kid."

Leona jumped up. She didn't want to hear Victoria talk about missing kids. Ike wasn't missing. Ike was hiding upstairs so his dad wouldn't find him. Leona was afraid that if she stayed in the kitchen, she might tell Victoria that Ike was upstairs in the closet. Then Victoria would tell Mom, and Mom would tell Mr. Boskowitz. If Mom told Mr. Boskowitz, he wouldn't be worried anymore, but then Ike would have to go.

"Don't worry about rinsing the dishes."

"Thanks, Victoria." Leona couldn't have rinsed anything right then. She couldn't even have carried her plate to the sink without dropping it. She ran out of the kitchen. She had to see Ike. She had to talk to him, except she wasn't sure what she was going to say. She had to warn him to be still or Albert might find him. But she had to ask him something, too. She had to find out if he had changed his mind and wanted to go with his dad. She had to tell him if he wanted to go with his dad, that was all right.

Leona shot up the stairs. The pancakes slipped out of her pajamas. She picked them up and brushed them off.

When she reached her room, she clambered into the closet. The box flaps were open. Leona fell to her knees. She held the pancakes in front of her and whispered. "I brought you some pancakes." She peeked into the box and dropped the pancakes.

"I don't want any more pancakes," Albert said from inside the box. He was holding a black marker and a folded page from a magazine. "What does that say?" he asked Leona.

Leona read the thick black letters written over the printed page. "TOP SECRET. That means it's important information. It's only for me." She unfolded the page. A message was written on the blank spaces of a mascara ad: "Sorry, Leona. I went with David. See you later. Ike."

Leona sat down in front of the box. "Ike's gone," she said to Albert.

"I know. We have to find him."

"No, I mean, Ike's gone home." Leona felt very tired, yet relieved, as if she had just swum a hundred laps. She stared at the closet wall.

"What are you looking at?" Albert said.

"The air," Leona answered. "I'm staring at the air. It's something you do when you are someplace else."

"But Leona, you are right here."

Leona shook her head. She reached out to hug Albert. "I know I'm here. I'm glad I'm here."

She got up and went to the back of the closet. "Ike forgot his suitcase, Albert," she said. "Let's go take it to him."

16

A Friend
Like Ike

They all went over to Ike's house, Mom and Daddy,
Victoria, Albert, and Leona. Leona pulled Ike's suitcase in Albert's wagon. Leona had opened the suitcase
and put one of her baseballs in it. It was the one Ike
had hit when they played in the park.

Albert sat in the wagon with his legs squeezed
around the suitcase. Leona had promised to pull him
if he would let her use his wagon.

"Leona," Mom said. "I think you should apologize
to Ike's parents. You gave them a scare."

"I didn't mean to," Leona said.

"That would be a good thing to tell them," Daddy
said.

"Gosh, Leona, did you really think Ike could live
in a box in our closet for the rest of his life?" Victoria
said.

"Of course not," Leona said. She didn't want to talk
about the secret plan she and Ike had thought up. It
wasn't going to happen now, anyway.

"I'm very fond of Ike," Mom said, "but I'm afraid

he couldn't live with us. His parents care very much about him, even if they don't live together anymore. Ike needs his parents."

"They need him, too," Leona said. She was thinking about how worried Mr. Boskowitz had been. "But I'm going to miss Ike."

"Me, too," said Albert.

Daddy looked very serious. "I understand what you mean about missing friends. I moved all the time when I was young," he said. "One of the worst things about moving was leaving my friends. I really missed them. But you know, wherever I went I met new friends."

"But Daddy, I'm not moving," Leona said. "Ike is. He will make new friends and forget about me."

"Are you going to forget about Ike?" Daddy asked.

"Never," Leona said.

"Ike's never going to forget about you either."

Leona knocked on Ike's front door. Ike came, and Leona handed him the suitcase. He took it and told them to come in. "I have to leave soon," he said. "David's almost ready."

Just as Rachel and Mr. Boskowitz slipped quietly into the room, Ike said to Mom and Daddy, "I'm sorry to have created such a disturbance."

"Me, too," Leona said to Ike's parents. "I didn't mean to scare you."

"It was very upsetting," Rachel said. "You can't imagine how I felt when I saw that Ike was gone."

"It's all right, Rachel. Everything is going to be all right," Mr. Boskowitz said.

Leona felt as if she had to be polite, especially after what had happened. What she really wanted to do was to go into the backyard with Ike and climb up the maple tree.

Ike was quiet, too, and serious, the way he had been before he played his cello at the gallery. Leona could understand. She knew that he was thinking about what his life was going to be like now. Neither of them talked much. Leona thought that sometimes good friends just need to be quiet together.

When she and her family had to leave, Leona held out her hand. "Good luck, Ike," she said.

"Thanks," Ike said, shaking her hand. "Thanks for everything."

Walking home, Leona realized that she hadn't even said goodbye. Neither had Ike.

"It's a letter for you," Victoria said. "From Ike."

Leona took the letter and sat down on the porch to open it. "It took a long time to get here. Ike's been gone for five days."

In the envelope was a folded letter and a piece of cardboard. Leona looked at the cardboard first. "Ike sent me a quarter," she said, and read the note on the cardboard: "I have two of these. It isn't real valuable but is in excellent condition. The date is 1949."

"Great," Victoria said. "So what's in the letter?"

"It's private," Leona said. Victoria shrugged her shoulders, but she didn't move. Leona got up and went into the house. She went upstairs to her closet, sat in the box, and turned her flashlight on the letter.

Dear Leona,

How are you? I hope you like this quarter. If you ever start collecting them, this can be your first. Try not to spend it.

Thanks for the baseball. I keep it in my cello case and take it out every day.

David took two weeks off work, and we are going to do lots of things together. Tomorrow we are going to buy an electric train. (I lied about the train. I never had one.)

I have special cello lessons twice a week and will start to go to a different school next week. It is for kids in the arts.

I wish you lived in the neighborhood. I miss you.

Your friend,
David Eisenhower Boskowitz (Ike)

Leona read the letter again, then folded it and put it back in the envelope with the quarter. She put it with her baseball cards in her lavender purse.

Then she wrote a letter to Ike.

Dear Ike,

      I like the quarter. It must be worth a lot. It's really old and is in good condition.

      I miss you. I never had a friend like you before. I hope you come in the summer. Mom says sometime we might go to visit you if it's all right. Daddy says he will take us to a White Sox game in the spring.

      Albert says he misses you, too, and Victoria says you are not really weird, you're sensitive.

      Write soon.

               Your friend,
               Leona Joan Hanrahan

Victoria told Leona to put the stamp upside down. That meant you sent a kiss with the letter. Leona was careful to put the stamp on right side up.

Leona rode her bike two blocks to the mailbox. She leaned close to the mailbox to listen as she dropped the letter in. It made a soft, satisfying plunk when it hit bottom.